I Just Had
To Go Back To
Di Island

Cover photo provided by William Torrillo, creator and photographer for the Old Mango Photo Guide to the U.S. & British Virgin Islands. William moved to the USVI in 2010 from South East Georgia. In Georgia, he worked as staff photographer for over 4 years at Sea Island Resorts, a Five Star Resort with over 80 years of history. Responsible for shooting resort rooms, activities, golf, aerials, food & wine, real estate, and content for publications and web. When not shooting commercial photography for clients in the Caribbean and South Florida, William posts daily photos of the USVI and BVI on the Old Mango Facebook page: www.facebook.com/Old.Mango

Located on the East End of St. Thomas, William provides professional photography services, graphic design, and web design to the USVI and islands throughout the Caribbean. William's website is: www.photo.vi and www.oldmango.com

**Mahalo and one love
as always to my family
and friends.**

**If you would like to visit
di Facebook island, go to
www.facebook.com/livelikeajimmybuffettsong**

Chapter One
"I went down to Crazy Chester's."

I had my toes in the water.

I had my ass in the sand.

And I, Jack Danielson, was bored.

Come to think about it, I should probably rephrase that. I was still living on di island, a beautiful tropical paradise filled with good people I had the even greater fortune to call my friends. I had a lovely girlfriend, Kaitlyn, who I got along with so well that I didn't need to think about how well I was getting along with her. And I owned a little rum factory that kept cruising along, even more smoothly without my help, that kept me in the flip-flop and tee shirt, boat drink and jerk chicken style I'd grown accustomed to.

Life was, in every way that mattered, good.

So if I was indeed feeling the slightest bit bored, it was due to the unnecessary but evolutionarily developed better the species trait that modern humans now have, which in my situation was about as useful as my little toe. There was nothing to better; my life, and the Earth in general, wouldn't be improved by my accomplishing much of anything. There was nothing in particular for me to do, except lounge around various gorgeous locations on di island, while talking to some very wonderful people whom I loved dearly.

So I guess I wasn't what I should really call bored, unless I wanted people who were in nowhere near my situation to throw small household appliances at my head in protest at my complaining. But I was waiting with a certain level of quiet, laid back, anticipation, for something interesting or at least different to happen around here.

Maybe part of it was that Kaitlyn wasn't nearby at the moment. She still hadn't committed to moving to di island permanently and was often away working, but I saw her enough that it felt just right. That is, when she came back, it felt just right; times like now I missed her. But she had every intention of settling on di island in the near future, and like everything else in our relationship I was just going to let it happen when she was ready, and not try and force it just because *I* was ready. She did, however, fill certain small gaps in my life, and when she was awol I had to fill them in other ways. And right now I wasn't having much luck with that.

I stood up, disconnecting my ass from the sand, and brushed the eastern beach off my bottom where it had gathered. I'd been watching Mother Ocean gently roll in and caress the Earth for about an hour, wondering if beaches weren't perhaps the planet's erogenous zones. Maybe that was one of the reasons we enjoyed lolling about on them so much, like a bunch of tiny little sandy minded voyeurs.

Normally I would have been doing my deep thinking back on my own beach, but it was still a bit noisy over there at times because of the construction during the final touches on the new nearby Wind Song Resort, due to open surprisingly soon. It seemed like just yesterday I'd been sticking bananas in Anderton Corporation's Jeep's tailpipes (yes, I stole the idea from Axel Foley), and today they were already filling up the pool. I guess time does indeed fly when you're having rum.

I followed the path that cut through the woods, and emerged on the road next to my electric golf cart. From the moment they'd finished paving a circle around di island and out to the high(er) traffic areas, I'd imagined tooling around on all that smooth new tar in my own cart, just like all those old dudes who used to putt past my condo on their way to the nearby country club. Not that I'd ever been much of a putter myself; I never really got golf, because like most beginners I'd sucked at it, and didn't see the point in making myself miserable while trying to learn not to. I was doing enough things in my life at the time that I didn't enjoy, and doing another one voluntarily and paying oodles of money for it didn't make much sense to me. Perhaps if they ever find a way to squeeze a course in here on di island I'll be willing to give it another whack or ten, since my happy scales are better balanced now. But hopefully they'll never fairway that much of my palm treed paradise.

I got on board my newest transpo device, turned the key, and pressed down on the gas pedal (of course there *was* no gas, but I kept calling it that anyway). The cart moved quietly and smoothly forward in an almost surrealistic way; electric vehicles may not yet have as much power as their smelly and noisy crude oil guzzling counterparts, but they did have a built in stealth feature that was fairly appealing. It felt almost like I was riding in something from a Harry Potter movie, propelled by some magical power I didn't truly understand but just went with. That is, until I'd hit one of those occasions where I tried to stretch the juice in the battery a little too far and slowly putted to a stop, at which time my cart seemed very Muggleish indeed. But if we couldn't still run out of gas, where would our love lives be?

I was fully charged this time though, and whisked south along the road. Ernesto passed me going the other way in his new old Chevy pickup and honked and waved, and I wondered briefly why he wasn't at the plantation, then realized he was probably picking something up from the southern docks. He took every opportunity to use his new truck, as did most of the drivers on di island; Mr. Wonbago told me that as of last week there were now twenty-seven vehicles between our shores. So yes, I guess we had a tiny bit of traffic. But no matter what Francis, the most interesting innkeeper in the world seemed to think, and stubbornly insist, I refused to agree there were enough cars to warrant drive-thru windows at di island restaurants. And that included his Monkey Drool's.

Which was where I wasn't headed and didn't soon arrive at, though I passed its friendly bamboo sign just before I rolled to a stop. Not that I wouldn't probably end up there eventually, if not for boat drink purposes, then to continue my diplomatic efforts in the cold war between the Innkeeper and Crazy Chester. So far, it had been so good, and I'd managed to keep any coconut missiles from launching. And though I'd had to put the U.N. Peacekeepers on high alert status a couple of times, crisis had eventually been averted, and overall I think Henry Kissenger would have been proud of me.

The problem was the building that I'd just come to check out the progress on. Situated a very short distance south down the beach from the Monkey, the bar with the big wooden deck on its roof was nearing completion. The interior and exterior would both continue to evolve as long as somebody brought in something funky to hang from its walls and ceilings, but otherwise only a few finishing touches on them remained. So it would only be a few more days until Crazy Chester's officially opened its doors to island and tourist revelers, and the Innkeeper's worst fears would likewise officially come true.

Chester and Akiko had finally made the permanent move here (Akiko *back* to di island) about eight months ago, shortly after Chester sold his old establishment in the Keys, Crazy Chester's Bar And Boat Stop. It hadn't been on the market very long before it went, to another former northerner from Montana who like me, had gone crazy and was making his own migration south. It had taken Chester a while to get over not owning his little one particular harbor; right up until the time his new one on di island had enough of a structure to place the six foot plaster mermaid he'd taken from CCBABS's above the entrance. I guess all it took was a little (well big, actually) bit of tail for Captain Crazy to feel at home again.

Of course, this new bar and restaurant of Chester's wasn't sitting at all well with the Innkeeper. Francis had been reveling in all the new customers who'd arrived since the start of the construction on the Wind Song Resort, happy to have a full place again after losing some of his crowd to Robichaux's. And now an even bigger libation outpost was cropping up a beach ball's throw away, so naturally he was a little annoyed. He'd been trying to come up with ideas such as the drive-thru window to top Chester's for months now, and had been feverishly mixing alcohols and juices together like a mad scientist in hopes of finding yet another perfect drink to go with his Pickled Parrot and Toasted Toucan. Because while the bar Chester was building was scary enough, what the Innkeeper truly feared was the great coming of the Chesterita that was soon to be unveiled next door. And maybe rightly so; it was one helluva drink.

I did manage to convince the Innkeeper that what with his Monkey Drool's, Robichaux's, and now Crazy Chester's all being situated on the same side of di island, the area had a chance of turning into a mighty entertainment mecca to rival the Vegas Strip (a bit of an exaggeration, but what the hey). That got him to promise to hold off on any extreme retribution measures until he saw the results. What was going to happen after that I had no idea, but at least Francis had stopped reading Soldier Of Fortune magazine every time Chester walked onto his patch of sand.

All I knew was that I myself could hardly wait for Chester's to open. The simple life on di island may have been great, but variety was also the spice of that life. There was nothing wrong with wanting to mix up my daily menu of just hanging about with a little metaphysical cayenne pepper, to go with all the other flavors that made my hours so tasty. Gumbo it up, I always say.

I waved at Miss Mermaid and walked beneath her through the open front door, and followed the sound of a hammer towards the main room. I found Crazy Chester there, hanging one of Jedidiah's paintings on the wall above the old retro jukebox.

"It's crooked," I said helpfully.

Chester jumped about a foot in the air, as he always did when someone sneaked up on him; for someone as laid back as he was, he got better air time when startled than a hot air balloon. When he landed back on Earth, he looked at the painting and said, "I know; I like it that way."

I shrugged. "Suit yourself," I said, nonchalantly, although I could hear my hands screaming at me with a primal need to reach out and level the ocean scene. I sometimes thought the pyramids were just someone neatly stacking a bunch of haphazardly strewn about stones that had been bugging them. "How's it all coming? I thought I'd stop by and see if you needed any help."

Chester stared at me for a second, as if surprised, then said, "As a matter of fact, I could use a hand. Follow me."

I'd been afraid Chester might actually take me up on my offer from the second it had slipped off my tongue, but I reluctantly tagged along across the wooden floor through the bar. The interior was very much like his old place in the Keys; woody, open, and eclectically decorated with anything pirate or sea related that seemed to be at hand. The tables were old barrels with tops installed upon them that were laminated over old faded photos, and the chairs a hodgepodge of mismatched furniture. A few wicker bladed ceiling fans slowly rotated above, sending a soft breeze through the room that lightly rustled the pirate and maritime flags that adorned many of the walls. All in all, it was already a welcome, homey, and nicely broken in atmosphere which hadn't even been broken in yet.

Chester led me up the stairs on the far side of the room, and onto the rooftop deck. I had a feeling that up here, under Sol with a view of the ocean, was going to be the popular place to be. Low tables with comfortable chairs were scattered about, each replete with a bright umbrella. Colorful lanterns hung up above them, strung from lines that ran between the tall poles from which hung even more flags along the railing. A tiki bar was situated against one of these railings, and across the floor against the other was...

"Is that what I think it is?" I said.

"If you think it's a stage, then, yeah," said Chester. "But if you think it's a hot tub, you're wrong."

"Why would I think it's a hot tub?" I said.

"Beats me; I'm just sayin'," said Chester.

"When did you build this?" I asked.

"This morning," said Chester.

"Been up since five again, have we?" I said.

"Four, actually," said Chester.

"Then you built part of it last night, 'cuz that's what four AM is," I said. Chester had a lot of strange habits that you might be able to call good, such as his no shoes, no shirt forever philosophy, but waking up before dawn had even considered cracking wasn't one of them in my opinion. "So who'll be playing here?"

"The Rum Powered Goats, of course," said Chester. "Three nights a week."

"All of them? Cavin, Boyd, Jedidiah, and Michel?" I said.

"And Moon Man," said Chester.

I paused to think before I spoke, making sure there wasn't a rum soaked memory lying about in my head I hadn't previously popped into a bottle, of meeting someone by that name. "Okay, I give; who is the Moon Man?"

"Not *the* Moon Man, just Moon Man; he's not sure he's the only one," said Chester. "And you'll meet him."

"I know that; it's di island, so it's kind of hard not to meet someone," I said. "But who is he?"

"He plays keyboard; he arrived here a couple of weeks ago," said Chester.

"Weeks?" I said, surprised. "Where's he been hiding all this time?"

"Communing with the sun," said Chester.

"Don't you mean the moon?" I said.

"Why would he do that?" said Chester.

"Because his name is...never mind; I don't want to know. How did you get all the other guys to play on a steady basis?" I said.

"I offered to pay them," said Chester.

"That might do it, I guess," I said. "Does the Innkeeper know you're going to have live music?"

"Yeah, I told him this morning," said Chester.

"Then I better stop in to the Monkey and hose him down or he's liable to spontaneously combust," I said. "So what did you need help with?"

Chester looked around him. "Can you pick up that piece of wood and bring it down stairs?" he said finally, while pointing at the floor next to me.

I looked down and spied a foot long, two inch wide chunk of lumber, then bent over and picked it up. "This?" I said, holding it up. "That's it?"

"Well, you never offered to help before and I didn't want it to go to waste," said Chester. "Other than that, I wanna do the rest with Akiko."

"Thanks for making me feel useful," I said. "Where is she, anyway?"

"At home, working on the menus," said Chester.

"So you're about ready then, aren't you? How long until you open?" I said.

"On Friday; I think," said Chester.

"Then I better get your rum supply over here," I said.

"Ernesto just dropped it off," said Chester.

"So that's what he was doing; sneaking around in that truck of his moonlighting as a delivery guy for the factory," I said. "Is there anything at all I can *really* do to help?"

"You could keep Francis next door from making his cocktails," said Chester.

That didn't sound very fair to me. "Come on, now; you've got the blenders lined up for your Chesteritas. He's got the right to make up whatever he wants, too," I said.

"Not if they're the Molotov ones he was talking about this morning," said Chester.

"Crap; I better get over there," I said, carrying my piece of wood with me as I hurried towards the stairs.

"And you might want to see if those hand grenades of his are going to be like the wet ones in the New Orleans' bars or like the exploding ones in Iwo Jima," Chester shouted after me.

I doubled my footly efforts, pushing the speed of my flip-flops to the very outside of the envelope.

A diplomat's work was never done.

Chapter Two
"Hearing Music For Free."

"Don't even try, Mr. Jack; we got noting to talk about," said the Innkeeper irritably, as I walked towards him where he stood behind the back outside bar at Monkey Drool's.

"Now, Francis-" I began.

"And how many times do I have to tell you not to call me Francis?" said Francis. "Only my mother calls me dat, and she be a helluva lot bigger den you. And what you be doin' with dat stick, mon?"

I looked in my left hand, and sure enough, the piece of lumber from Chester's deck was still riding along there. I hid it behind my back, and said, "Never mind that; I came to tell you you can't burn down Crazy Chester's bar."

"You don't tink so? Den you just sit back and watch; you'll see. Dey will be able to see di flames from di passing cruise ships," said the Innkeeper. "Dey will tink der's a bonfire on di beach, and dey will be right."

"You tell them, Innkeeper!" said Willie, toasting Francis from his barstool with his Coca-Cola.

"Don't encourage him; he hardly needs it," I said, as I sat down next to Willie at the bar and kicked off my flip-flops, something I now did without thinking (both the sitting down at the bar and the kicking off). "Look, Innkeeper, we've talked about this; having another bar on di island is gonna be good for everyone."

"Ya, ya, I've heard it all before; di more places der are for di tourists to come and visit, den di more tourists will *come* and visit," said the Innkeeper. "You been babblin' about dat for weeks."

"Well, it's true," I said. "Ask anyone in Key West."

"And di band next door? How many of dose same tourists are gonna wanna sit here when dey have di music right over der?" said the Innkeeper, leaning over the bar towards me and pointing in the direction of Chester's. "How is dat gonna help me?"

"Um," I said.

"Ya; not so sure now, are you?" said the Innkeeper. "All those Goats up on di roof makin' all dat racket."

"They will be, won't they?" I said, thoughtfully.

"Ya, mon, for sure," said the Innkeeper.

"And you and your customers will be able to hear them plain as day," I said.

"Dat's what I be sayin'," said the Innkeeper, grumpily.

"Great for you, eh?" I said.

"Ya, right!" snarled the Innkeeper.

19

"No. Great for you, eh?" I said.

The Innkeeper leaned forward again and narrowed his eyes at me. "What'cho mean, mon?" he asked.

"Don't you get it? Free music," I said.

"Free music?" said the Innkeeper, puzzled. Then you could see a tiki torch fire up in his head, and he smiled broadly. "Free music! We be havin' free music here!"

"You got it," I said, relieved.

"Dat idiot, Chester; he'll be payin' dose guys to play, and I be gettin' it too, for free!" said the Innkeeper. "Dat's what he gets for building so close to me."

"I guess so," I said. "Unless of course you'd like me to try and convince him not to have a band."

"No, no; it be okay wit me!" said the Innkeeper, quickly. "I tink it will work out for di best."

"Glad to hear it," I said.

The Innkeeper reached into one of his coolers, pulled out a Kalik, opened it, and sat it on the bar in front of me. "Dis one be on me; I got to go to di back and work on some tings," he said, happily.

"Thanks," I said, and Francis patted me on the shoulder and disappeared inside.

"Phew," I said.

"Nice one," said Willie, clinking his Coke bottle against my beer.

"I always figure if I appeal to his sense of greed I might have a chance of averting disaster," I said. "But I'll be glad when Chester's opens; I'm running low on maybes, half truths, and white lies."

"You don't think he'd really set Chester's on fire anyway, do you?" asked Willie.

"I'm not so sure about that; ask Jedidiah some time about the great plantation fire, when the workers struck back against the mon," I said.

"I will," said Willie. "Sounds like it was an interesting time."

"It was something, all right," I said, recalling the resulting shotgun pointed at my noggin'.

Willie was just a fifteen year old kid, but he seemed wise beyond his years. He'd been on di island for about a year now, having escaped from Cuba along with three older friends; they'd been aiming for Puerto Rico and had somehow missed it, ending up on our shores instead. His buddies had eventually continued on, but Willie had stayed, saying that if this was where he had ended up then maybe it was where he was meant to be. And in any case, he was happy to be free wherever he was.

He missed his family of course, but it was his parents who'd insisted that he leave when the chance finally came in the first place. They'd also seen to his education, making sure he spoke a very fluent English (probably better than my own Americanese, as a matter of fact). It seemed to me if there were more parents in the world like Willie's there would be a lot less to try and escape from in the first place.

"I've actually got something I've been wanting to ask *you* about," said Willie.

"Oh?" I said, picking up my Kalik and taking a sip, enjoying the fact that there was enough tropical heat to already make it sweat a little.

"Yes," said Willie. "I hate to; my father told me to never in-debt myself to anyone. But I'm not sure what else I can do."

"Do you need help with something?" I said. "Some money, maybe?"

"Yes; I do. Have you seen the old van that Mr. Wonbago drives around in?" said Willie.

"I know he hates it," I said. "He told me it was beneath the dignity of a public official like himself to not drive something nicer, like a BMW. Or a Cadillac. Or a truck with *really* big tires."

"That's the one," said Willie. "Well, he found a truck with *really* big tires in Anguilla, and now he wants to sell the van. And I'd like to buy it."

"Do you mind my asking why you need a vehicle in the first place?" I said. "The minute they paved the road everyone around here started thinking about getting something to drive on it in, including me, I guess. But nothing's any farther away than it was before, so..."

"But I don't want it just for me to get around in," said Willie. "I want to start a taxi service."

"A taxi service? Really?" I said.

"Yeah; I've got it all worked out. I already talked to Jolly Roger, and the Innkeeper, and Henri over at Robichaux's," said Willie. "And the manager at the Wind Song."

"It sounds like a great idea," I said.

"But that's not all; I want to sell cards to the tourists that give them a discount at all the bars," said Willie.

"*All* the bars? Do we have enough on di island to start talking about them as an all?" I said.

"We have five now, if you count the bar at the resort and at your rum factory," said Willie.

"Five bars," I thought to myself. *"When the hell did that happen?"*

"But I need to get your permission to put the rum bar on the cards, too, of course," said Willie.

"How did you get Mr. Stingy, the Innkeeper, to go along with it?" I said.

"Well, for one thing, each bar gets one dollar from every card I sell," said Willie.

I figured that probably hadn't been quite enough for Francis. "And?"

"And I told him his place wouldn't be on the taxi bar tour route if he didn't take part," said Willie.

"Didn't occur to him that you'd be stopping at Crazy Chester's right next door to Monkey Drool's anyway, eh?" I said.

"I guess not," said Willie, with a shrug.

"So did you need money to buy the van, then?" I asked. "How much does Wonbago want for it?"

"I've got some of the money; I just need another five hundred dollars," said Willie, hopefully.

"No problem; it sounds like a very good idea. The tourists are always bitching about the walk to the factory, and I'd gladly pay that much just to make them shut up," I said. "I'll tell Faith to write you a check."

"Thank you; I'll pay you back as soon as I can," said Willie.

"Just put the dollars you were supposed to give to the factory for the bar cards in a coffee can, and when you get five hundred of them you can give me that, and we'll call it even," I said.

"B-but you'd be getting those anyway," said Willie.

"It doesn't matter. The way I see it, you're going to be helping *us* out by bringing people in," I said. "All the bars should be paying to help get a taxi service started." And besides; Willie reminded me of Cavin, and taking a chance on him at the factory had been a blessing waiting to happen.

"Well, thanks, Jack," said Willie. "You won't regret it."

"I know," I said. "That's why I'm doing it."

"G'day, mates!" said a voice from behind me. "Would this be a good place for a bloke to hit the turps?"

Chapter Three
"That's When I Came To Meet My Australian Friend."

"What?" I said, as smartly as usual, to the tanned, bearded man in the beat up cowboy hat.

"Can an ocker get a pint of grog here?" said the man.

"I think he wants to know if he can get a drink here," said Willie.

"The nipper there's got it," said the man, then he walked over to us and stuck out his hand. "Cooper Walker's the name," he said.

I shook his hand, which I noticed was very rough, and said, "I'm Jack Danielson, and this is Willie."

"Pleased to meet you gents," said Cooper, while tipping his hat ever so slightly at us. "Mind if I pull up a stool?"

"You can sit here," said Willie, standing up. "I've got to go tell Mr. Wonbago I'll take his van. And I need to see if Gus is anywhere on di island."

"If you mean that bushranger Gus Grizwood, he might be at some Cantina place; that's where he was headed when I flew in with him an hour or so ago," said Cooper.

"Thanks," said Willie. "And thanks again, Jack; I appreciate the help."

"No problem; I'll try and stop by the factory later so you can pick up your check tomorrow," I said. I watched Willie until he disappeared around the corner, then turned to Cooper where he now sat on the barstool next to mine.

"So where's the keeper of this boozer?" said Cooper.

"He's in the back somewhere," I said, and then shouted, "Innkeeper!" When Francis still didn't come out, I started to get up, and said, "I'll go get him."

"Keep your seat; I reckon he'll turn up. I know these islanders; got their own way of doin' things. Like me," said Cooper.

"So where are you from, Cooper?" I asked. I was pretty sure I knew the answer, but I'd been wrong before. And while guessing someone was from Iowa when they were from Wisconsin usually didn't do too much harm to public relations, mixing up your Irish, Welsh, Scottish, English, Aussies, and Kiwis was a different matter entirely. One that at the very least got you off on the wrong foot, as if you'd stuck it in your mouth all the way up to your boat shorts.

"Call me Coop," said Cooper. "And I'm from the lucky country, of course. Especially since they have me to brag about."

"And that lucky country is..." I said.

"Australia, mate," said Coop. "Down under. I'm a sandgroper, to be precise."

"I'm more of a sandsitter, myself," I said. "I've never really had any thoughts of groping it, although I do run my fingers and toes through it from time to time. But overall, the sand and I have more of a platonic relationship."

Coop ignored my attempts at humor and continued. "That just means I'm from the Western part of Oz. I was born in Bunbury, down on the coast."

"So what brings you to di island? Vacation?" I asked.

"You mean, besides that crazy bloke, Gus, and that wobbly plane of his? That's top secret, at least for now," said Coop with a wink. He had a grizzled face, more grizzled even than Grizwood's, with twinkling blue eyes; sort of like a Santa Claus who lived in the Sahara Desert instead of at the North Pole. "But I can tell ya that I'm not just here to sunbake."

Just then Francis finally emerged from inside, holding a pitcher in his hand. "Ah, sorry, mon. Didn't know anybody was out here waitin'," he said.

"Innkeeper, this is Coop Walker. Coop, this is the most interesting innkeeper in the world," I said.

"Welcome to my Monkey Drool's!" said Francis, beaming one of his best host smiles. "I be di Innkeeper, like Mr. Jack says. What can I get for you?"

"What's good here?" asked Coop.

"The Parrots and Toucans are good," I said. "Try one of those."

"Hey, great you say dat when you do; I've been in di back trying to mix up a new concoction to go wit dem. Do you wanna try it?" said the Innkeeper.

"I'll give it a shot," I said.

"Why not?" said Coop.

Francis grabbed a couple of coconut mugs from under the bar, filled them from the pitcher he was carrying, and handed them to Coop and I.

"Cheers, mates," said Coop, and he and I each took a long drink.

I considered my options for the next few seconds, then looked over at Coop to see what he was doing and found him grimacing as if he'd been kicked in the family jewels by a kangaroo. "Do you have a name for this thing?" he said at last, holding up his mug.

"Not yet," said Francis. "Any ideas?"

Swallowing finally won my contest in a close race over spitting, and I forced myself to do just that. "How about calling it *"Dead Buzzard That's Been*

Laying By The Side Of The Road In The Sun For A Week?"' I said.

"Dat might be hard to fit on di specials sign," said the Innkeeper.

"And a tad bit too complimentary," said Coop.

"Not so good, eh?" said the Innkeeper.

"Not so good," I said.

"I was afraid of dat," said the Innkeeper, then he shrugged. "I was tinkin' dat might not be di right new direction to take. Oh, well; back to di drawing board."

"How about a pint to wash that down with before you go?" said Coop.

"A Red Stripe okay?" said Francis.

"Anything; I'm feeling strangely un-picky right now," said Coop.

"Do you want another, Mr. Jack?" said the Innkeeper.

I took one last pull on my Kalik, finished it, and stood up. "No, thanks. A guy like me's got a lot of important things to do, so I better get at 'em," I said. "Nice meeting you, Coop. Are you going to be on di island for a while?"

"As long as it takes, mate," said Coop. "As long as it takes."

"Then I guess I'll be seeing you around," I said. "G'day to ya!" I added, unable to resist.

I wandered back to my cart and drove off to do my important things.

And a half hour later, I was fast asleep.

Chapter Four
"Governor Of Somewhere Hot."

I woke up from my afternoon nap next to my ocean and stretched luxuriously, then rolled expertly out of my hammock, onto my feet, and into the sand below. I wriggled my toes in the tiny grains a bit before slipping them back into my flip-flops, and if that qualified as groping, so be it. Then I walked up the hill away from my tiki shack and towards my little rum factory; it was time to do number two of my important things for the day, having just woken up from doing number one.

There were a few touristy looking folks having a bite or sampling some rum (or both) on the deck, as well as a smattering of locals doing the same. I said hello to a few of them as I passed by, then made my way into the factory itself, and stopped as usual to take it all in.

Di Island Rum Company really was a thing of beauty these days. Since I didn't have a whole lot to spend the profits on, I'd been using some of them to further spruce the place up. Not a huge amount of money by any means, but it was amazing what some brightly colored paint and a few decorations could do. I didn't see why a factory floor couldn't be almost as aesthetically pleasing as a quaint and quirky little island pub, and I was proud to feel that I'd proven my point.

I found Faith in her office, busy as always with paperwork. As someone who's work life consisted mostly of wandering around waiting for someone from the factory to actually need me for something, a rare occurrence to say the least, I was constantly amazed how everyone else employed by the factory seemed to have a full plate of duties to perform. The only time my plate was full was when Boyd served me my Jambalaya at Robichaux's, and even then it didn't stay full for very long.

I cleared my throat, and Faith didn't even bother to look up.

"Not now, boss," she said, continuing to page through a stack of bills.

"How did you know it was me?" I said.

"You're di only one who wouldn't just walk in and shout, *"Hello, Faith!"* You're still too polite for di island life," she said.

"I suppose I'm still used to tip-toeing around whenever I go into my boss's office," I said.

"I'm not your boss, boss," said Faith.

"Yes you are; you know it, I know it, and everyone else around here certainly knows it," I said. "But I'm good with that."

"Den what can I do for you so I can get back to work?" said Faith.

"I just came by to tell you...well, ask you, since I don't want to get fired, to write a check for five hundred dollars to Willie," I said.

Faith stopped what she was doing and looked up at me. "For what?" she said.

"He wants to buy a van," I said.

Faith sighed loudly, apparently exasperated with me yet again. "Boss, you are way too nice with your money; do you have any idea how much di islanders owe di factory?"

"I have no idea," I said, since I didn't.

"Well, it's a lot," said Faith. "Roger owes you money, Boyd owes you money, Michel owes you money, Jedidiah owes you money...even Mr. Wonbago owes you money."

"Why does Wonbago owe me money?" I asked.

"Because he knows he can," said Faith. "You give di only interest free loan on di island, so everyone keeps borrowing from you. If we ever have a money problem we are going to have a money problem."

"I thought everyone was pretty good about paying us back," I said.

"Dey are," said Faith. "But den dey just borrow from us again."

"Are we really that tight on cash?" I said.

"We're tight enough dat if someting big broke down round here dis month, our funds would get pretty darn low fixing it," said Faith.

I hadn't realized we'd gotten to that point yet, mostly because I paid no attention to it. Then again, it did seem like people had been asking me for money fairly often lately, mostly when I was in a celebratory mood, probably because they knew I had a tendency to say yes to just about anything at that point. "Okay; I'll have to learn to say no for a while," I said.

"Thank you," said Faith. "We should be fine again if you give us a month or two."

"I will; after Willie," I said.

Faith gave me the closest thing she had to a glare in her arsenal.

"I already said yes," I said, almost pleading. "And besides; his is for a good cause."

"If you say so," said Faith. "Five hundred?"

"Yes," I said. "He'll stop by for it sometime soon, I'm sure; he's pretty gung-ho."

"Speaking of stopping by, Pat wanted you to come and see him," said Faith.

"Probably wants to try and sell me that treadmill desk again. I keep telling him I don't *want* to exercise and I don't *have* anything to work on, and he keeps saying everyone can use a good workout and I could use the desktop for a bar and drink while I walk.

Evidently he's unaware that exercising while relaxing is just the sort of real sin the devil is waiting for you to commit; never mind fornication and imbibing, this one will get you the hot seat for sure," I said. "And don't even get me started on the *"Everyone can use a good workout"* comment."

Faith just continued to stare at me.

"Just shut up and leave, right?" I said.

"Someting like dat, boss," said Faith.

"On my way," I said, and left the office before she could wing her Swingline at me.

I decided to leave my golf cart at the factory, since I was already tired of riding it for the day. I was beginning to regret buying it; it had seemed like a good idea at the time, and Pat had done a great Toasted Toucan sales job on me at Monkey Drool's the night I'd ordered it from him. But it was something I didn't really need, and I'd begun to miss my walks across di island.

There was something special about slowly hoofing it through a tropical environment, and as I meandered down the road towards the Crossroads and Pat's sporting goods store, I enjoyed being in rhythm with the leisurely pace of di island once again. Not that my cart was likely to take first place at Talladega, but riding it here was still like having a speed metal drummer in a reggae band. Everything in life has its proper tempo, a song to be played a certain way. And charging back and forth across di island was just wrong; passing under a palm tree was a thing that should never be rushed.

Thankfully Faith, and Cavin for that matter, went right back to being the same laid back islanders they used to be the moment they finished their faster paced work day; I wouldn't have been able to live with myself if it had turned out to be any other way. How could I come here to escape the stress of the mainland, only to end up creating stress of my own for other people to deal with? Talk about your heavy sins. I know it's all just a part of modern life, but it wasn't a part I wanted to have a hand in spreading.

At the very least I was certain that the factory had done far more good than harm. And despite all my worries about any changes that might come with the building of the Wind Song Resort, it actually felt like di island was just reaching its peak. There was now an even more pleasant balance here to life between the new and the old, the newfangled and the primitive. As a former citizen of so called civilization, I liked the fact that I could now sit under an old thatched roof on one of my favorite stretches of deserted beach, and have a piping hot pizza delivered to me by moped. I'd always known I'd been in the right place; it was only lately I'd come to realize it was at the right time, too.

And often the time you are in a place is even more important than where that place is.

When I got to the place I was going to be in right now, the Crossroads, I found it to be as bustling with people as always. It had definitely become a daytime tourist stop favorite, what with all the little gift shops peppered around the area, as well as the Cantina and the new Coral Reef Pizzaria. And of course, there was always Hoser Pat's Sporting Goods, in case you felt the sudden urge to work off all those pina coladas.

Pat still wasn't exactly getting rich from hockey stick sales, but he was making a decent living renting out scooters and bicycles to the tourist crowd. It was a tough racket, though; that same slow, easy pace I enjoyed always took a while to seep into the minds of visitors, and when their asses hit a scooter seat they instantly became a wild pack of Evel Knievals. There was many a time a bike came back looking like it had been run through a picket fence or two, which it sometimes had. Insurance or no, it had to be a pain in the ass.

I'd been tying to talk him into renting out diving equipment, but he was still in the think about it phase. I didn't know why he was lolly-gagging; there were a number of coral reefs around di island and other great underwater vistas to explore, and sooner or later someone was bound to beat him to it. I was surprised as it was that no dive instructors had made di island their home, but so far the market was still open for Jacque Cousteau wanna-bees.

I found Pat out in front of his store as usual, kneeling down and cleaning up one of his rentals. He was as pink as always; Pat never tanned, and the tropical heat made his Canadian skin look like Canadian bacon. But he loved his life on di island as much as the rest of us, in spite of all his profuse sweating and rose colored outer shell. Maybe he had rose colored pupils as well, hiding behind his Canuckian greens.

"Hola!" I said.

Pat looked up and smiled at me, then gave the bike one more quick wipe and stood up. "Hola yourself," he said. "Have you ever noticed that *"hola"* is *"aloha"* spelled backwards, but without the A?"

Besides being the pinkest person on di island, Pat was also the one most filled with useless facts, sometimes so useless they didn't entirely make sense. "No, I can honestly say I never noticed that; maybe I better start holding up phrases in front of the mirror to make sure it doesn't happen again," I said. "Faith said that you were looking for me?"

"That's what I like about you, Jack," said Pat. "Always straight to business."

"I wouldn't go that far, unless it's to get it out of the way," I said.

"Well, let's get it out of the way then," said Pat, heading towards the front door of his store. "Follow me."

I did so, through the standard commercial glass and metal door, and was hit by a wave of cool, conditioned air. Pat's place was one of the few such ice boxes on di island (except for the new resort, of course), and it always came as a bit of a shock to my system to feel it again. I had to admit, it felt kinda good, though. I'd grown accustomed to the heat of the tropics and didn't mind it; hell, I loved it most of the time. But occasionally being cool and comfortable didn't entirely suck, either.

Pat went behind his check-out counter, a glass case where he kept his display of island beach balls and Frisbees for those last minute impulse buyers, and knelt down. Then he stood up, a big cardboard poster in his hand, and said, "Ta-DA!"

I stared at it and blinked, wondering which one of us had lost his mind in the frigid cold.

"So, what do you think?" asked Pat.

"It's me," I said.

"Yes it is," said Pat.

"On what looks like a campaign poster," I said.

"Yes; for governor of di island," said Pat. "Do you like it?"

I wasn't sure how to respond at first. The idea of me running for any office was strange and out of the blue enough to begin with. But seeing myself in my best palm frond hat, sunglasses, and flowered shirt, rum drink in hand, above the phrase, *"Kick back with Jack; Jack Danielson for governor of di island"* was just plain weird.

"Which part would you like me to talk about first?" I said. "Do you want me to critique it as a work of art, or as an idea who's time hasn't come?"

"Either or; we figured you'd for sure at least like the laid back campaign slant," said Pat. "You see, the thing is, with all the expansion on di island lately, we feel it's time to have a government in place."

"There goes the neighborhood," I said. "And you think for some reason that I'd want to be the one heading said intrusion on all the sanity around here?"

"Myself, and a few other people, yes," said Pat.

"Well, you and your few other people thought wrong," I said. "In the first place, the last thing I want is more responsibilities."

"But you told me a few days ago that you don't *have* any responsibilities," said Pat.

"Yes, and I want to keep it that way," I said. "Anyway, if I did want some, responsibilities that is,

I'd choose doing something more useful than being a politician, like training coconuts to play dead or something."

"I see," said Pat.

"Why do we suddenly need a government, anyway? We've been getting along fine without one; more fine than the rest of the world, in fact. If we need to work something out, we usually just do, and if we can't, Wonbago figures it out for us," I said.

"And that's the problem; Mr. Wonbago's been getting a little out of control lately. You could even say he's downright power hungry. You remember what happened with the Wind Song; he pretty much made the decision to sell the land to Anderton without even asking anyone else, and he's been doing similar things ever since. It's just too easy for him to do whatever he wants right now," said Pat.

"If you elect a governor it's just going to be the same thing, only with whoever you vote in, instead," I said.

"Yes, and that means we're obviously going to have to write some laws, too, to keep everything in check," said Pat.

"Well, good luck with all that," I said. "You can count me out; when you paved the road, you just got cars. But if you go making laws, you're going to get lawyers. It'll be like throwing chum in the water, except the sharks that come to feed will all be wearing three piece suits and Rolexes."

"That's too bad; I guess we're going to have to find someone else," said Pat, obviously disappointed with me.

"Why don't you guys just get Wonbago? At least he wants to be in charge," I said.

"He's already running for the office, but we wanted an opposing candidate," said Pat.

"First I've heard of all this," I said.

"That's because you don't exactly keep yourself informed about the important things on di island," said Pat.

"Yes, I do; I know if someone is having a party, where all the hammocks on di island are, when and where the Rum Powered Goats are playing, and how low I can go at a limbo stick without hurting myself," I said. "What else is there to know?"

"Fine; keep your head stuck in the sand," said Pat. "I'll tell them you said no."

"Yes; you tell *them* I like my ostrich way of life," I said. I took one last look at the poster and turned to leave, then reached back and snatched it out of Pat's hand and walked out. I thought it would make a nice souvenir, and a reminder that the only person who truly knows who you are and what you want is you, so you better keep a keen eye out or they might end up making you governor one day.

And what a step down that would be from the Big Kahuna.

Chapter Five
"There's A Moon Man In The Jungle."

A few days later I was in semi-seclusion. It turned out the *them* who Pat had said wanted me to run for office included a large number of islanders, and they were being as good-naturedly stubborn about the matter as always, pestering me to change my mind every time I ran into one of them. Usually I eventually caved in and let them have their way, but I wasn't about to do it this time. So I'd been more or less hiding from everybody and sticking to some of the quieter places on di island, hoping the whole thing would blow over like a tropical storm.

Of course, it wasn't easy avoiding people on di island. Today I was hiking all the way up to Black Dog's Peak just to get away; it had been a while since I'd seen my uncle Billy anyway, and it seemed like a good time to try and hunt him down. Especially since all the places he was likely to be were places everyone else was likely *not* to be.

Black Dog's Peak was the highest point on di island, near to my uncle's pirate hideout. It was a little clearing on the top of a hill, and you could see most of di island from its summit. It was also the place where Billy's cannon was located, the one I used as a signal whenever there would be a beach party at my hut that evening. But it hadn't gone off in a few days, since there was no need to throw a fund raiser to fill the coffers of my non-campaign.

When I got to the summit and looked around, I found my uncle sitting cross-legged on the ground in the middle of the clearing, his back to me. Or so I thought at first glance, until I looked at him more closely. The man seated there did have long, graying hair just like Billy, and was wearing a pirate type renaissance style shirt, too. But his was a brightly (albeit faded) tie-dyed colored one, something no self-respecting buccaneer would be caught dead in, unless they were trying to lure the opposing ship's crew in to a love-in. And the small, round-lensed, turquoise colored shades perched on his upturned face were hardly Captain Blood approved, either.

I approached the man slowly, going in a wide circle around the clearing until I was standing in front of him, then cleared my throat. Although I remembered what Faith had said about my being too polite for the tropics, this guy didn't exactly look like an islander, and I felt that mainland etiquette should still therefore apply. When he didn't respond, I ventured a tentative, throw caution to the wind, "Hello?"

"Just a minute, man; I'm almost done," he said, without otherwise moving.

I waited patiently, glancing occasionally upwards to see what he might be looking at. There wasn't much to see; just your standard issue, bluer than blue Caribbean sky, a few sea gulls, and Sol. Pretty, but personally if I wanted to stare at something for any length of time, I'd stick with my ever changing, blue-green ocean any day of the week.

"Amen," the man said finally, then he stood up, and brushed the dust off himself. "Fully charged for the day."

"That's a relief," I said.

He was tall, taller than me, standing about six foot three, but very thin. He had a good sized scraggly, graying, beard, and spoke in a slow, laid back manner, reminiscent of California or playing a vinyl LP at the wrong speed. I guessed he was probably somewhere in his late sixties, but it was hard to tell with the shades and all the hair. My thoughts were that he resembled a low budget B-movie wizard, my opinion of which was reinforced when he bent over and picked up the tall, gnarly, wooden staff that had been laying on the ground next to him.

He leaned back and looked at me, running his fingers through his beard absentmindedly. "Let me guess," he said finally. "You're Jack, right?"

"Yes; yes I am," I said. "How did you know that?"

"Cuz you *look* like Black Dog, man," he said.

"I do?" I said. I'd never really thought I resembled my uncle; to me, we didn't even look like we were related.

"That, and you've got the tattoo he told me about," he said, pointing at my arm.

I looked down at my right appendage, and there it was; the little treasure map on my forearm leading to di island with the phrase, *"I have found me a home."* I'd had it done one night by Graciela, a lovely Brazilian senorita who had set up a tattoo and hair parlor in the Crossroads. "Oh yeah," I said. "That might be a dead giveaway."

"But you do look like your uncle, too, dude; at least through the eyebrows, anyway," said the man. "I'd know them anywhere."

"I'm going to take a wild guess here myself, and say that you're Moon Man," I said.

"Right on, brother!" said Moon Man, smiling warmly.

"So what were you just doing?" I asked. "If you're Moon Man, I would think you'd be sitting under Luna, instead."

"Oh, I do that too, every once in a while. But to shine like the Moon at night, I need to absorb some sunlight during the day," said Moon Man.

"And that makes you glow?" I said.

"It makes my aura shine, yeah," said Moon Man.

"Then does everybody's aura who lays out in the sun glow at night?" I asked.

"No, man; it's not enough to just hunker down under Sol here on Mother Earth. You've got to be one with the sun if you want it to soak in more than skin deep. You gotta let it into your soul, you know? You need to free your mind and let it float away into the cosmos where it can really get zapped by the rays," said Moon Man dreamily.

"And that's what you were doing when I arrived? Floating out in space?" I said, doubtfully.

"Yeah; I was waaaaay out there. You should try it sometime. It's like, totally radical," said Moon Man, leaning on his staff.

"I'd give it a whirl, but I'm afraid of heights," I said.

Moon Man shrugged. "Suit yourself, brother."

"So I take it you've already met my uncle Billy?" I asked.

"You mean, *Captain* Billy Black Dog; yeah, I met him. Again, you know?" said Moon Man.

"I know every part but the again," I said.

"I knew Captain Black Dog in the old days; back in Key West when he was just Billy. Those were some wild times," said Moon Man. "But I had to meet him again when I got here to di island, this new Black Dog dude."

"How did you know he was here? Or was it one of those cosmic coincidences that keep happening on di island where you just showed up and found him?" I said.

"No, man, I ran into Black Dog's groovy lady friend over at the Schooner Wharf Bar one night; we got to talkin' and somehow Billy came up, and she told me he was hanging out here. I guess the whole thing *was* kind of out there," said Moon Man, thoughtfully. "Anyway, I said to myself, "Dude! We should go see Billy!" And I decided to listen to myself, and we did, so here I am."

I'd always wondered about Billy's past, and Moon Man fit right into what I'd imagined when I combined the sixties, seventies, Key West, Jamaica, and boat loads of ganja. And I assumed the lady friend Moon Man was talking about was the one who'd had Billy smiling and singing a bawdy pirate song when he came back on board the next morning during our visit to Key West a while back.

"Are you going to be staying on di island for a while?" I asked.

"Until it's time to move on, amigo," said Moon Man.

"And how will you know when that is?" I asked.

"I'll know, man; believe me, I always know," said Moon Man. "Like we all should know, you know?"

"I know," I said, and almost did, which kind of frightened me. "I should be moving on right now, too, as a matter of fact. I'll be seeing you around, though, I guess; you'll be playing with the Goats, won't you?"

"Yeah, I play with the goats from time to time," said Moon Man. "It's good to commune with nature, and goats are pretty cool furry little dudes."

I thought about that; Boyd was a little furry, but...

"No, I mean the Rum Powered Goats," I said. "You know, at Crazy Chester's?"

"Aw, yeah, man; *those* dudes! Yeah, we'll be jamming together on Friday," said Moon Man. "It's gonna be groovy."

"See you then, then," I said, turning to leave.

"Uh, what day is it today, amigo?" said Moon Man.

I stopped and had to ponder that for a moment. "Wednesday; at least I think it is."

"Riiiight," said Moon Man. "Thanks; saved me checkin' the stars."

"Glad to help," I said, and headed towards the path back down the hill.

"Keep on truckin'!" Moon Man shouted after me.

Moon Man enjoyed sitting out under the sun and stars, liked goats, didn't know what day of the week it was, and could probably out laid-back attitude even an islander.

I had a funny feeling he was going to fit in perfectly around here.

Chapter Six
"Nephew Of A Sailor."

I didn't find my uncle until the next day. Actually, the next evening; I found he and Sam sitting on his shipwrecked old boat, the Rum Runner, which still lay washed up on on the beach north of the Coconut Motel. I didn't know how much longer it would be able to remain there, however; it was unfortunately becoming a favorite spot for tourists who'd reached the higher plains of inebriation to play, which wasn't exactly pleasing Billy. It was either move it somewhere safe, for both the ship and the boat drink drunks, or risk Captain Black Dog shish kabobbing some kid from Wisconsin on spring break.

Tonight though, the coast seemed clear; it was Thursday, and di island always seemed quieter on a Thursday. By then, most visitors had gone back to the Virgin Islands to prepare for their weekend flights home. Of course, there was a chance all that would change in the near future; with the new resort nearing completion, there was now serious talk of building a small airport somewhere on the north end of di island, near my Sugar Daddy Plantation. In fact, it was an almost certainty as long as a parcel of land big enough could be found, which didn't look to be much of a problem. When it did happen, we'd be fully connected to the outside world, reachable from anywhere in a matter of hours. Oh well, say la vee.

I boarded the Rum Runner and petted Sam, my uncle's Black Lab and first mate, then sat down in the chair next to Billy in the back of the boat. He was quiet; too quiet, having only acknowledged me with a weak wave as opposed to his usual rousing pirate greeting.

"Ahoy, Captain!" I said, finally, when he continued to just sit there.

"Ahoy," he said, somberly.

"What's the matter, Black Dog; you don't seem like yourself tonight," I said. There were times I could call my uncle just plain Billy, or even uncle, and he'd respond, but never on board his boat. On the Rum Runner he was a pirate captain, and that was that. "Has someone been messing with your ship, again?"

"Aye; probably," he said, staring over the shore out to the ocean's waters, a grim look on his face. "But I'll be dealin' with that later. Right now, I've got bigger things on me mind."

"Care to talk about them?" I asked. "Maybe I can help."

Captain Billy Black Dog turned to look at me. "You, lad? I don't think so," he said. "If me problem had to do with dancin', eatin', or lolly-gaggin' around on the beach, then I might come to ya for help. But when pirate matters matter, you're about as useful as a termite in a peg leg."

Obviously it was going to be one of *those* conversations with Billy. "How do you know I can't do anything to help until I have a clue what the problem is?" I said. "Maybe it affects one of the other pirates on di island, too, for example, and I could at least get a message to them for you."

"I don't think you're ever going to have a clue, laddie," said Black Dog. "But I've got to admit, it be true what you be sayin'; you are good at flappin' your gums. So maybe you could warn Jolly Roger, at least. And maybe that scurvy sea dog, Captain Crazy."

"Glad to be of service, as always," I said, dryly.

"I know you are," said Billy. He turned his chair and leaned forward, as if to conspire with me. "You know the new blaggard what's been skulkin' around di island?"

"You mean Moon Man? I thought he was a friend of yours," I said.

"Not him, ya landlubber!" said Black Dog. "I'm talkin' about that throw the shrimp on the barbie, black hearted cur who flew in with that other snake, Gus Grizwood, in that contraption of his."

Captain Billy Black Dog Danielson got along well enough with most people now, even his old rival Crazy Chester who he was for the most part friendly with. But Gus and his plane were another matter. I guess the old Noorduyn aircraft didn't fit into Billy's pirate world, so he wasn't about to cut Gus, its pilot, any slack, either. "You mean, Coop Walker?" I said. "Yeah, I met him; he seemed alright. What about him?"

"Aye, I saw you two gettin' cozy at the Monkey a couple of days ago," said Billy.

"We talked for like ten minutes!" I complained, wondering where Billy had been so that he could have seen us.

"Long enough to hatch any plot," said Captain Billy Black Dog. "The only reason I'm trustin' you now is he seems far too clever to fall in with the likes of you."

I knew my uncle loved me; he'd let it show on the rare occasion. But tonight he was keeping it locked tightly in a chest, hidden somewhere down in the crushing depths near Davey Jones's level. "Fine; but if you want my help, let's just stick with the facts."

"I never said I wanted yer help; I just don't have any other choice," said Black Dog.

"Would you just tell me what's going on?" I said. "What about Coop?"

"Do you know why he's here on di island?" asked Billy.

"No; no I don't," I said. "He told me it was a secret for now."

"Well, I do," said Billy. "He's after me treasure."

I sighed. Sometimes my uncle Billy sounded like Lucky the Leprechaun; someone was always after his Lucky Charms, or so he'd say. "Now what makes you say that *this* time?" I said.

"Because the scoundrel told me so!" said Billy.

"You talked to him? But you don't talk to anyone, unless you know them. Or unless you're on vacation with us drinking a lot of rum," I said.

"I didn't want to, but I didn't have any choice," said Black Dog. "He invaded my hideout."

"He did?" I said, surprised. "When was this?"

"Yesterday, a couple of hours after I saw you try to sneak up to the peak and fire my cannon without me permission; luckily me old mate Moon Man was there to stop ya," said Black Dog. "Anyway, I was just sittin' there mindin' me own business in me cave, wonderin' which rum most needed me gullet's attention, when the blaggard just strolls right into me lair! Damn near ran him through, I did."

"What stopped you?" I said.

"I gave him a chance to plead for his life, and he apologized, so I let him live; for now," said Billy. "But I don't think he meant it. He kept snoopin' around me cave, and I finally had to chase him out. I'd be up there guarding it right now, 'cept I happen to know he's over at the Monkey."

"Did he tell you what he was doing up there?" I asked.

"Aye, and that's the problem," said Black Dog. "He's after me treasure, I tell ya. Oh, that's not what he said, of course. He says he's on di island lookin' for the treasure of some other buccaneer named Roberto Cofresi, but I know better."

"Roberto Cofresi? Who's he?" I asked.

"That's what I said, too lad; never heard of 'em. And if I never heard of him, he can't have had much in the way of plunder to hide. I'm sure it's just some imaginary pirate he made up so he can skulk around and search for a real pirate's treasure. Namely, mine!" said Billy.

"But don't you remember? Jolly Roger and I dug up your treasure a couple of years ago; the one under the double X's," I said.

"That ain't the only buried plunder I have, ya rumskull; I never much saw the intelligence in hidin' all me swag in one spot," said Billy.

"Maybe Cooper figured since you were a ghost and long dead you don't need it anymore," I said.

"Well, he figured wrong; dead wrong, if he doesn't watch it," growled Billy.

"You're sure that's what he said, though; that he's here to search for treasure?" I said.

"Aye; I may be dead, but I'm not deaf," said Black Dog.

"Then I suppose I better go talk to him," I said, standing up. It seemed like I was always going somewhere to talk to someone about something these days.

"Talk to him?! I didn't tell you about it so you could go talk to him. I told you so you could go warn the other pirates, 'cuz he's bound to be after their loot, next," said Billy.

"I'll do that, too, but only after I find out all I can from Coop; I want to see if I can learn exactly what he's up to," I said.

"I just told you what he's up to!" complained Black Dog. "But I suppose you're right; you are a sneaky little bastard, so you might as well stick to what you're good at."

I ignored yet another of Billy's insults and started to leave, then stopped. "Damn; I wanted to chat with you about your old friend, Moon Man, and the old days."

"What's to talk about? He's me old mate, and he's here. If you want to know anything else, ask him. I don't go gabbin' about everyone behind their backs like you do," said Billy.

"I don't go...well, okay, maybe I do a little, from time to time. But it's just a habit I picked up from di islanders," I said. "It's a national pastime around here to talk about your friends and neighbors on the Coconut Telegraph."

"You all could learn something from us pirates; we know a thing or two about keepin' our traps shut. That is, unless we're spillin' our guts to stay clear of Jack Ketch and his hangman's noose," said Black Dog.

"I'll try and control my every urge to gossip in the future," I said. "Unless I get captured, that is." I patted Sam one last time, and disembarked from the Rum Runner.

My uncle Billy's mood and personality swung back and forth from day to day like a tavern sign in a typhoon. Sometimes he wasn't that much different than the rest of us; maybe a bit insane, but weren't we all? Tonight he was back in full pirate mode again, more so than I'd seen in a long time.

Hopefully it wasn't a lighthouse beacon warning of dangerous seas ahead.

Chapter Seven
"Off To See The Monkey."

As I approached Monkey Drool's I could see there was a good sized crowd out back, made up mostly of islanders. That too was typical for a Thursday evening, which had become the unofficial day for the rest of us to meet at the Monkey once most of the tourists had gone home, or at least, homewards.

"Jack!" Pat shouted at me as I grew nearer. "Come over here; I want you to meet the newesht candidate for island governor, before he fallsh flat on hish face."

It seemed like Pat was the one who was about to fall flat on his face, wobbling around as he was like a buoy on rough seas. I walked over to him, looking for Coop as I went, and said, "I'm gonna need a boat drink if I'm going to be subjected to any politics."

"Here; take my Parrot," said Pat, handing me his coconut mug. "I don't think I need any more tonight."

I managed to take the mug from Pat before he could drop it into the sand, then took a sip, and said, "That's better. Now where's this new candidate you replaced me with?"

Pat put his hands on his hips and stood up as straight and proud as was possible with the high octane racing boat fuel he had for blood, and said, "You're lookin' at him."

"You? You mean, you talked yourself into running?" I said.

"Yep. I ashked around, and no one elshe seemed interested, sho I decided to do it myself," slurred Pat. "I've been chelebrating all day."

"I can tell," I said. "So do you have a campaign slogan yet?"

"I was thinking about "Vote for Pat, ya hosers!" said Pat. "What do you think?"

"I think what it lacks in originality is made up for by the fact that no one around here is gonna get it anyway," I said.

"Perfect! I'll shtick with it, then. And since I've got you right here, right now, let me run a couple a thingsh by you I've been thinkin' about to make thingsh better 'round here," said Pat. He started to open his mouth, then he stumbled a bit, burped, steadied himself, stumbled again, blinked, and finally said, "On second thought, maybe thish candidate should just go fall down somewhere, hopefully in hish bed."

"That sounds like a great way to make things better around here," I said.

Pat reached out unsteadily and patted me on the chest. "Glad we're on the same page, Jack" he said, then he took off in the not so general direction of his cottage.

"Smooth skating," I said, then watched as he weaved his way through the crowd, and then across the open sand, even though there was nothing else to weave around at that point.

"Thank god he's finally gone," said Jolly Roger. "He's been driving everyone crazy for hours with all his ideas on how to improve di island."

"How about by leaving it alone?" I said.

"Dat's what I said, too," said Roger.

"Are you going to vote for him?" I asked.

"No way, mon," said Roger.

"So I guess that means you're going to vote for Wonbago," I said.

"No way, mon," said Roger.

"You're not going to vote for anyone? But it's your civic duty," I said, parroting what I'd been told back in the states during numerous elections.

"Why? If I vote for one of dem, I'm saying I want dem to be my governor. But I'm not gonna lie," said Roger.

"Good point," I said. "I never thought of it that way. Anyway, the last thing I want to talk about right now is politics. Have you seen Cooper?"

"Ya; he's up at the bar. He said he likes to stay near di action," said Roger.

"Thanks; we can talk later about why we're not voting for who we're not voting for," I said. I went up to the bar and did indeed find Cooper there, engaged in a lively conversation with Gus.

"Well, look what just washed up on shore," said Gus. "Here's the guy you wanna talk to, Coop. If anyone's got any kind of control over Captain Billy, it's Jack."

"I wouldn't go that far," I said. "But if you have a problem with my uncle, I am the one to talk to. Of course, my answer for you would probably be to just leave him alone."

"You're talkin' about what happened up in the cave yesterday between your uncle Billy and me, aren't ya?" said Coop.

"Yes; he just told me about it," I said. "So you tell me; are you really looking for lost treasure like he says?"

"I am indeed," said Coop. "And my research tells me it may have been hidden somewhere right here on di island, by the Puerto Rican pirate Roberto Cofresi."

"And this Cofresi really was a pirate?" I asked.

"Yes, he was. In fact, he's a legend in Puerto Rico, and parts of Latin America; there's even a town named after him in the Dominican Republic. They say he was like a Robin Hood, sharing his plunder with those in need," said Cooper.

"And you think he buried some of that plunder here on di island?" I said.

"That's what all the signs I've found point to," said Coop. "It's at least certain he sailed in these waters."

"Is that why you were poking around in Billy's cave?" I asked. "You have reason to think it might be in there somewhere?"

Cooper took off his cowboy hat and scratched his head. "Well, to tell the honest truth, I'm not sure exactly where on di island it is," he said. "But there's a cave in Cabo Rojo, Puerto Rico, where they say Captain Cofresi used to hide his treasure, so it makes sense he might use a cave again, here."

"If that's the case, then knowing Captain Billy Black Dog, he's probably already found the treasure and claimed it as his own," said Gus. "I doubt he'd even tell anyone about it if he did."

"That's true; for all I know, my uncle's got a fortune in gold doubloons hidden in his parrot cookie jar," I said.

"Any chance you can talk to him and see if he knows anything?" said Cooper. "And if he doesn't, could you ask him if I could come inside and take a look around without having my life threatened?"

"I'm not making any promises, but I'll see what I can do. It's gonna be a toughie, though; Black Dog doesn't like intruders, especially in his hideout," I said.

"I'd appreciate the effort in any case, mate," said Cooper.

"No problem," I said. "Hey, by the way; is it just me, or were you talking differently here at the bar a couple of days ago when we first met?"

"Oh, do you mean something like; that galah, Pat, was sure doin' some earbashing tonight, wasn't he? That dill was as full as a goog. I reckon he'll be doin' the technicolor yawn later, eh? What a whacker," said Coop.

"It sounded almost totally undecipherable like that, yes," I said.

"Yeah, I can lay on the Aussie slang pretty thick when I want to," said Coop. "I used to talk like that all the time, but now I usually just do it when I want to be more colorful."

"It sounds almost like a second language," I said. "Ernesto wanted to teach me Spanish once, but I told him I didn't see the point since I hadn't mastered English, yet. And anyway, I didn't feel the need to walk around telling people I was grateful they were my best cheeses while I practiced."

"Your attention, mon!" shouted the Innkeeper, suddenly. "I need a volunteer. I have a new drink to go wit di Pickled Parrot and Toasted Toucan for someone to try," he said, holding up a pitcher.

A hush fell over the crowd, and everyone suddenly found their footwear to be utterly fascinating, looking down to avoid catching the Innkeeper's eye. Word had gotten around quickly, as the word always did on di island, about the quality of Francis's newest concoctions, and nobody was anxious to sacrifice their taste buds on the altar of science tonight.

"Oh come on, mon; dis one's gonna be good, I tell ya," said Francis.

Di islanders remained silent; you could have heard a drink umbrella fall into the sand, if Jimmy hadn't been singing about a lone palm on the boom box behind the bar.

"Oh, hell; give me one," growled Gus, finally. "I can't stand all the tension in the air. Wussies."

"Thanks, Gus," said the Innkeeper, while filling a mug from the pitcher.

Gus took the coconut from him. "It can't be worse than some of the stuff I've subjected myself to over the years. Bottoms up!" he said, and bravely (or foolishly, depending on your point of view about such things) took a good, long drink from it.

We all waited with bated breath for his reaction; there wasn't much that passed for a dramatic moment on di island, and this was about as suspenseful as it got around here. And just when the tension reached a point that would have had most New Yorkers, well, falling asleep with boredom, Gus finally let out a satisfied sounding, "Ahh."

The Innkeeper looked at him expectantly. "Is it good, mon?"

Gus milked it a bit, knowing all the attention was on him for the moment, then said, "Excellent. A little pineapple, a little coconut; kind of reminds me of a Painkiller. But I could taste some other things in there, too, that makes it very different. What are they?"

"Dat be a secret I'll be keepin' to myself," said the Innkeeper with a big smile.

"Well, you did good," said Gus. "What's it called?"

Francis held the pitcher high in the air, like a newborn baby, and said, "I hereby name dis drink, di Cockeyed Cockatoo!"

"Great name," I said. "Can I get one?" I asked, sliding my now empty coconut mug across the bar.

"Oh, sure; now that you know it's safe to consume you're all over it," said Gus.

"Hey, you weren't here for the Dead Buzzard the other day," I said. "I'm surprised my taste buds didn't shut down for good after that one."

"I'll vouch for that," said Cooper.

"Dis one be on di house too, Mr. Jack, if you can tell me if it's as good as Chester's Chesterita," said the Innkeeper, while filling my mug.

"Deal," I said. I took a tentative sip, just in case Gus was pulling a fast one and it actually tasted like another avian piece of roadkill. But I had to admit, it was good. I took another, bigger drink, and changed my assessment to damned good. "Gus is right; it is tasty. I don't know if it's as tasty as a Chesterita, because it's different, sweeter, but I'd say it's just as tasty."

"Dat be good enough for me!" said Francis, happily. "A free Cockeyed Cockatoo for everybody!" he shouted.

I thought for a brief moment the Innkeeper might just fill up one mug and have the crowd pass it around and share it, but against his penny pinching nature, he actually mixed up one for each and every one of us in the bar. Maybe it was so we could all try it and get hooked, or maybe he was trying to be generous on the eve of Crazy Chester's grand opening tomorrow afternoon. All I know is it definitely got the party rolling, and it didn't end until the wee hours of the morning.

I remember the festivities moving on to my tiki shack for a bonfire, Cavin raiding my rum factory for more rum, a long, rowdy, conga line, someone getting naked (as always, and even more unfortunately as always, it was Gus), and that same, naked person trying out the Wind Song Resort's recently filled pool next door.

I don't remember my outside hammock looking very inviting, which it evidently did at some point, and I don't remember stealing Coop's hat, which I woke up wearing in said hammock the next morning.

And I really didn't enjoy Cooper's rugged face staring down at me during that wake up, grinning from ear to ear.

Chapter Eight
"Doubloon As Big As The Ritz."

"Wakey, wakey," said Coop.

"Ugh," I said, which described both the way I felt and my view of Coop.

"Here; drink this," he said, practically forcing a glass into my hand.

"What is it?" I asked, sitting up as much as I was able to in the hammock. "My eyes aren't open enough yet for me to identify it on my own."

"It's a Bloody Mary; I took the liberty of making you one from your tiki bar. The way you were snoring and slobbering all over yourself, I made a wild guess and figured you were gonna need it," said Cooper.

"I wouldn't have needed it if you hadn't woken me up," I complained. "That's one of the joys of being me; I don't have to get up until my body is good and ready and regenerated enough to do so. What are you doing here, anyway?"

"You don't remember, do you?" said Cooper. "You said you wanted to go treasure hunting with me this morning."

"This morning? That doesn't sound like me; must have been evil, stupid Jack," I said.

"Well, whichever one of ya it was, I'm here now and you're awake, so drink up," said Cooper.

I took a drink of the Bloody, and it immediately added some moisture to my mouth, which had been about as dry as the sand below me.

"Better?" asked Cooper.

"Yes," I said.

"Good," said Cooper.

"Still very bad, though," I said, and I laid back down and closed my eyes. "Come back in three hours; that's my estimated time for recovery."

"You told me you'd do this, too, and that I should ignore you and get you up no matter what it takes," said Coop.

"People change, and I'm not the person I was last night," I said. "If I had to guess, I think I might have been Al Roker."

"I'm afraid you're getting up, and that's all there is to it, mate," said Coop.

"You wanna bet?" I said. "I'm laying here now, and I'll still be laying here two hours from now; there's no damned way I'm gonna be moved."

Two hours later I was trekking down a narrow path through the northern woods, sweating Toucans, Cockatoos, and Parrots out of my system with every step. It turned out that if a hammock is spun entirely upside down that even I couldn't stay on board, no matter how deeply dug in I was. My stomach and head were on the road to a full recovery after a swim in Mother Ocean and a Cajun style shrimp and gator omelet at Robichaux's, as well as a Mango Daiquiri to further ease the pain. They still weren't what I would call happy with me, but then I wasn't happy with me, either. I had a lot of kissing up to do with myself, and it might be a while before I was on speaking terms with me again.

I didn't know where we were going (Coop and I that is, not me and I). That didn't bother me so much, but I wasn't sure that Coop knew where we were going, either.

"Do we have some destination in mind, or are we just taking a stroll in the heat and hoping we trip over a treasure chest?" I asked, as I followed along behind my fearless Australian leader.

"Yeah, I know where we're going, more or less," said Coop.

"You want to let me in on it?" I said. "You could at least tell me how you know where this more or less place is."

"I have some maps," said Cooper.

"Can I see them?" I asked.

"No, mate; they're top secret," said Coop.

"If you ask me, there's way too much about this treasure hunt of yours that's top secret," I said, pushing a branch out of my face. "I get the feeling a lot of it's even top secret to you."

"Are you sayin' I don't know what I'm doin'?" said Cooper.

"No, I think you know exactly what you're doing. I just don't think you know exactly where you're supposed to be doing it at," I said.

Coop stopped in a small clearing in the brush and wiped his brow. "Look, mate, if I had my way we'd be up in your uncle's cave, but you said you needed to talk to him first," he said. "So I'm checkin' out a few other possible places on di island."

"I kind of assumed that, at least," I said. "My question was how you know what we're looking for, and what the thing that you know we're looking for is, so I can look for it, too."

"Okay; if it'll make ya happy. I recently came into possession of a very old book. I don't know if I'd call it a diary or ship's log, really; it's more a collection of notes and drawings," said Coop.

"And where did you get this very old book?" I asked.

"E-Bay," said Coop.

"E-Bay!" I said. "Known for being a reliable source for pirate treasure hunting information, are they?"

"I know, I know," said Cooper. "But the guy didn't know what he had; he'd picked it up on vacation at a flea market in St. Kitts, and was just trying to make a few quick bucks."

"So what was in this flea market E-Bay book of yours that has me trudging through the jungle today?" I said.

"The most important things were the initials and a year; R.C. and 1823, which fits the time frame Roberto Cofresi was active. That, and there were some crude maps with notes and more dates," said Cooper.

"And these were treasure maps, you think?" I said.

"Possibly; some of them, anyway," said Coop. "But to be honest, it's hard to tell with most. A lot of them could have been anything; places he visited, areas with supplies he might need..."

"So we might be sweating our asses off and being eaten by bugs while stepping over snakes, all in search of Captain Cofresi's long lost favorite island tiki bar?" I said.

"Possibly, yeah," said Cooper.

"Then it better be open when we get there," I said. "So is there anything in particular we're looking for? Some kind of landmark?"

"This clearing, for starters," said Cooper.

"This tiny thing is on the map?" I asked.

"More precisely, that statue," said Cooper, pointing.

"What statue?" I said, turning to look. Then I said, "Well, I'll be damned."

It was just a small gray stone really, about two feet tall, and crudely carved. Whoever had chiseled at it hadn't exactly taken the time to turn it into the next Venus De Milo; it was about as detailed as Frosty the Snowman after an hour or two of tropical heat.

"That was marked on one of the maps; it goes a long way in proving that Captain Cofresi was at least on di island," said Cooper.

I shrugged. "Maybe," I said. "But the journal just says R.C.; it could just as easily have been that R.C. Cola was the first true cola, and they were here searching for Kola Nuts."

"Always the doubter, eh?" said Coop. "Well, the world needs those too, I guess. Come on; let's see what lies up ahead."

We continued to follow the trail, if you could call it that, forcing our way through the woods. I'd started to go down this path once during one of my island walkabouts, but had turned around when the quality of the road quickly deteriorated, becoming as much of a joy to be on as an Illinois highway. I had no idea where Coop and I were by now; the trail had twisted and turned so often I couldn't tell if we were going east, west, north, or down. For all I knew, we were about to pop out next to my tiki hut, which would have pleased me to no end since I could have fired up the Frozen Concoction Maker.

Finally we came to another, slightly bigger clearing, and stopped. I took a look around, and said, "Maybe you are on to something."

"What makes you say that?" asked Cooper.

"This old building. Well, leanto, I guess. Maybe your pirate camped here," I said.

"Maybe; this all looks way too recent, though," said Coop, as he poked around, lifting up old pieces of wood and decaying straw mats. Then he leaned down and picked something up and tossed it to me. "Or maybe it was *your* pirate who passed through."

I caught what Coop threw to me, and turned it over. It was heavily faded and mildewed, but I could still make it out. "Sports Illustrated Swimsuit Issue, nineteen seventy-three," I said. "Yeah, this could have been Billy; I don't think he's ever missed an issue. I wonder if this spot is where he first stayed after he crashed the Rum Runner."

"All I know is this is where the map ends, so there's supposed to be something important here," said Cooper, continuing to look around. "And just because your uncle may have been here doesn't mean Cofresi couldn't have been, too." He pulled his metal detecting wand out of his backpack, and started, well, detecting, I guess.

I walked round and around the little clearing, checking out every little thing I came across. I wasn't searching for signs of Cofresi's lost treasure, although Coop had been right when he said there was something important here. But we had different reasons to think so; for Cooper, it was his search for pirate plunder. But for me, it was because this little glade may have been the place of origin of that other, more notorious pirate. My uncle, Captain Billy Black Dog Danielson.

I finally sat down on a broken log in front of a fire pit in the center of it all, perhaps inhabiting the same seat as Billy once had, and tried to imagine him being here. If it had indeed been right after his shipwreck, he wouldn't have been in a very good state of mind, especially since the sinking was what seemed to have sent him off the deep end to begin with. His original first mate and Black Lab, Sam, would have recently been lost at sea, and Billy would have probably felt very much alone. And seeing where this lost little clearing he'd chosen to hide was located, he'd evidently wanted to be as far away from other people at the time as possible.

We're constantly changed by events going on in our lives. Sometimes they're cumulative and chip away slowly at our psyche, like yet another bad day at the office, or another smile from a pretty girl that raises our confidence. But occasionally something happens that alters us in the blink of an eye, and we instantly become a different person, for better or for worse. My uncle's shipwreck was such an event, and in the aftermath, perhaps while sitting where I was right now, he'd become someone else; part Billy, and part Black Dog.

I heard Cooper's metal detector start making a sort of *"whoop-whoopity-whoop"* sound, and he said, "Found something." I stood up and walked over to him on the far side of the clearing, as he pulled a shovel out of his backpack.

"What is it?" I asked.

"It's a metal detector, not a metal identifier; we have to dig up whatever it is to find out," said Coop, and he began to do so.

"If it's a coffee can filled with Babe Ruth rookie cards, it's Billy's, and I have dibs," I said.

"I think I'd know those weren't Cofresi's," said Coop. "He'd have had Roberto Clementes."

"How much you want to bet it's something like that, though," I said. "Maybe a hubcap off an old VW bus, or a bag of brass doorknobs, or-"

"Or maybe a chest of gold doubloons," said Black Dog.

He stood on the opposite side of the clearing, leaning against a palm tree, dressed in full pirate regalia. It was hard to tell by the look on his face what kind of a mood he was in; he didn't look angry, but then, he didn't look overly happy, either.

Cooper stopped digging for a moment and stood up, perhaps waiting to see what would happen next, something I know I was doing. When Billy did nothing other than adjust his tri-corner hat, I said, "Do you want us to go, Black Dog? We can just leave whatever it is there."

"Ya want it so damned bad, ya might as well dig it up. It's all yours, now, lads," said Billy.

I wasn't sure what to do, but Cooper was, and he began to dig again. Now that my uncle had appeared I wasn't surprised that he'd been hiding nearby watching us; he had a knack for knowing when someone was anywhere near his territory, especially me. But what did surprise me was how calm he was being about the whole thing; I myself had had a nagging feeling all morning that Cooper's search might lead to trouble. Which may have been why the evil Jack/Al Roker had wanted to come along today in the first place, to keep an eye on things and be there if Billy did indeed show up.

It wasn't long before the soft Earth gave way to something more solid, which I heard the shovel head bang against. Coop knelt down and dug feverishly with his hands, and soon pulled a relatively small, old, wood and metal box from the hole. I glanced over to see Billy's reaction, but just like that, he was gone again.

I knelt down next to Coop, and he and I looked at each other, and then at the box. There was no lock on it, just a latch of sorts to keep it closed. Cooper reached out very slowly and, just as slowly, opened the lid, then looked inside.

"Stones. Lots and lots of stones," said Cooper, obviously disappointed for some strange reason.

"Sorry, Coop," I said.

"They aren't even interesting ones," said Coop, digging through them. "Not an agate or piece of quartz in the whole lot."

"I take it there was nothing in your research about Captain Cofresi being a rock hound?" I asked.

Coop looked at me. "Funny," he said.

"I try," I said, and looked back at the box. "Wait a minute; there's something stuck in the lid; it looks like an envelope." I carefully reached out and pulled it free.

"It better be an I.O.U. for treasure," said Cooper.

I turned it over in my hands and checked it out. It was small, the sort of envelope you might use for an invitation or to put on a gift. I opened it slowly and pulled the card out from inside, and read it.

"Well?" said Cooper, finally.

"You're not going to like it," I said.

"I already don't like it," said Coop.

"Then you're not going to like it more," I said.

"What is it?" said Cooper.

"It's your I.O.U. for treasure; sort of," I said. "It says, *Captain Black Dog was here.*""

"What?!" said Coop, snatching the card out of my hands. "That yobbo stickybeak whacker!"

"Feeling colorful again, are we?" I said. Then I checked the envelope once more, which felt heaver than it should have. "Wait a minute; there's something else in here." I reached in and pulled the something out, and held it up.

We both stared at it for a moment, as it glittered in the sun.

"Is this what I think it is?" I said. "Or is it a chocolate dollar wrapped in foil?"

"No, that would have melted by now in this heat," said Cooper. "Let me see it."

I handed the coin to him, and he examined it closely. "1806; Charles IV. Looks like a genuine, gold, Spanish doubloon, alright," he said. "Fits Cofresi's time period, too. And he did attack Spanish ships late in his career; led to his downfall, in fact. This is great, mate!"

"It is?" I said.

"Of course! Don't you see? It's obvious your uncle found Cofresi's treasure, or part of it; maybe in this very box. Then he probably hid it somewhere else, and left this annoying little note," said Cooper, smiling ear to ear.

"Maybe; or maybe Billy happened to have a Spanish doubloon he came across somewhere and an old box and decided to play a joke on whoever dug it up," I said.

"I don't know; I don't think so. There's too many coincidences. This spot, the year on the coin, all that," said Cooper. "And what would've been the point of the whole thing?"

"You don't know my uncle," I said. "I think that's just the sort of thing he might do, especially since it's pirate related."

"You can say what you want, but I'm not giving up this easy; even if it is just a prank, that doesn't mean there isn't a real treasure hidden somewhere on di island," said Cooper.

"Well, I am giving up, at least for today," I said, standing up and brushing all the dirt of my person. "It's getting late-er, and I have a grand opening to go to."

"If that involves a coldie at a boozer, I'm right beside you, mate," said Coop.

"Mine is gonna involve a Chesterita on a rooftop, but you gotta do what you gotta do," I said. "Come on; let's get back to civilization."

Chapter Nine
"I Have Found Me Another Home."

"She cook gumbo, A mighty rad gumbo! It's the only way she can go, down at the Club Rad Gumbo!"

The Rum Powered Goats were jamming up a storm on Crazy Chester's rooftop, and the mixed crowd of locals and tourists were loving it. They especially seemed to be grooving on Moon Man, who was turning out to be a helluva keyboard player. They cheered every time he went into one of his crazed solos, his long hair flying all over the place as he bobbed his head madly to Boyd and Jedidiah's bass and percussion rhythms. As did Cooper, hopping around on the dance floor in front of the stage like a drunken kangaroo to the Little Feat tune.

The Goats weren't the tightest band ever to hit a note, but that didn't matter. They were good enough, and anything they lacked in pure musical ability they more than made up for in enthusiasm and that good, live music sound. Di island did the rest, providing the finest accompaniment of tropical sounds, smells, breezes, and temperatures that any musical act could hope for. I could probably sit and listen to the Jonas Brothers for hours if they were on a beach somewhere. Probably. Okay, maybe not, but you get my point.

I picked up Chesterita the Fifth off the bar and carried him over to Roger's table and sat down next to he and Jolly. "What do you think?" I asked.

"About what, mon?" asked Roger.

"About the bar, the band, the Chesteritas; about everything," I said.

"I tink di Innkeeper be in trouble," said Roger.

"You know, I don't," I said.

Roger looked at me, puzzled. "You don't like dis new place?" he asked.

"No, that's not what I meant," I said. "I love it here already, and it's gonna be great having a new place to kick back in. But Monkey Drool's will always be Monkey Drool's. It's the prototypical, beat up old weathered, stand in the sand while you drink various feathered friends next to the world's ugliest stuffed monkey beach bar. That area is just way too saturated with good times for people not to keep going back. People like me."

"I suppose you be right," said Roger. "I can't imagine never being at di Monkey again; just tinking about it makes me want to stand up and go der right now."

"We should, later," I said. "I looked down over the railing a few minutes ago; there were some people there, but no islanders. We should stop in just so Francis knows we still love him."

86

"And di monkey," said Roger. "We can't forget to love di monkey."

"No we can't," I said. "Maybe I'll steal his sombrero again and wear it; I haven't done that for a while."

A great bar can become a best friend, or at the very least, a second home. I remember what it was like when I was young, back when I was a fun person before I became the un-fun person I'd had to become fun again to chase away. There was a local pub that my friends and I used to hang out at that was the unofficial center of our universe. Beer, music, girls, pool, sports, and friendship, everything a human needed to be human, they were all there. And then suddenly it was gone, forced out of business when four chain bar restaurants with deep corporate pockets moved in nearby.

We tried a couple of other spots in town, but it was never quite the same. All our good times had been left behind in our old haunt, and the new locations didn't have any memories. If you ever want to hear and see it summed up musically, watch Jimmy Buffett's *Bama Breeze* video some time; it's clear Bubba understands just how much a bar can mean to you, and it ain't just about the drinking.

Chester hurried over to the table next to us and delivered a plate of coconut shrimp, then plopped down on one of our chairs. "I need a break," he huffed.

"A little bit busy, are ye?" said Roger.

"Yes; too busy," said Chester. "I'm better and happier bein' a host than waitin' on people; I don't like em *that* much. I'm gonna have to hire some help, especially servers. I get the feelin' anyway that for some reason people would prefer having their food brought out to them by a cute girl or guy rather than an old fart wearing just a pair of swim trunks."

"I'm funny that way, too," I said. "The last thing I want is chest hair in my Conch Chowder."

"Ew, mon," said Roger.

"I was kind of surprised you even decided to serve food; I mean, your illegal mahi-mahi sandwiches back in the Keys were great, but I thought you might keep it simple here," I said.

"Akiko's too good a cook, and she wanted something to do, anyway," said Chester. "And people expect it nowadays."

"I guess so," I said. "The days of the bar bar are numbered. Great job with your place, though; I think everyone loves it."

"Thanks. But I better get back to it; don't want some whiny tourist to wait an extra minute for their damned Jerk poppers," grumbled Chester.

"Good luck," said Roger.

Chester trundled off, and I said, "Poor Chester. All these danged people showing up at his bar, sitting around spending money. He's a victim of his own success."

"Maybe he should trade bars with di Innkeeper," suggested Roger.

"You're right; he might be happier. I know if I owned a bar I'd want it to be like the Monkey; nice and easy," I said.

"Maybe you should open a beach bar, too, Jack," said Roger.

"A rum factory's not good enough, eh?" I said. "I make di rum and I drink di rum; might as well have a place to serve it, too?"

"I'm serious," said Roger. "You'd make a great innkeeper."

"I'm not sure how well that would go down with Francis, not to mention Chester now, here," I said. "Besides, I already have a bar, up at the factory."

"I don't know if I'd call dat little grill in di corner of di patio a bar," said Roger.

"Maybe not," I said. "But still; I've got enough going on already."

"Ya, you're obviously worked almost to death," said Roger.

"It's not easy being me," I agreed.

The Goats finished their set, and Cavin and Moon Man came in our direction as they left the stage. "Hola, dudes!" said Moon Man. "Can we hunker down here with you?"

"Pull up a seat," I said. They did so, and I said, "You guys are sounding great tonight; the keyboard really adds to the band. I'm guessing you've been playing for quite a while, Moon Man?"

"Just a couple of hours, man; no big deal," said Moon Man.

"No, I mean, overall; in your life," I said.

"Oh, yeah, for sure!" said Moon Man, brushing the hair out of his face. "I've been groovin' for a long time. I played all over Key West back in the day, you know?"

"Did you ever play with Jimmy Buffett?" I asked.

"Yeah; probably," said Moon Man. "I don't really know for sure; those days are kind of a blur. You know how it is; playin' acid rock 'til you're numb. But I'll keep an eye out for him the next time I have a flashback I know's gonna come."

"Wait a minute; isn't that from a Buffett song?" asked Cavin.

"Is it?" said Moon Man.

"Yeah; *We are the people our parents warned us about,*" I said.

"You mean the dude stole my lyrics?" said Moon Man. "What a bummer."

"Jimmy Buffett stole your lyrics?" said Cavin.

Moon Man looked upset, then broke out laughing. "No, man! I'm only fooling. I probably did know the guy, though; I just don't remember. There's a lot of things I don't remember, for some reason."

"Maybe it has to do with frying your brain," said Pat, who'd walked up beside our table.

"Oh, man! Go away, dude," said Moon Man.

"What's the matter?" I said.

"This guy is the man, man!" complained Moon Man. "Always bringing me down with his politics. And he's from Canada! I didn't even know they had politics in Canada."

"Of course we do!" said Pat. "And it's just as important here on di island."

"I can't listen to this; it'll ruin my karma," said Moon Man, getting up. "I'm outta here."

"I'll go wit you," said Roger.

"Me too," said Cavin.

"Cowards!" I said.

The three left, and Pat said, "Guess it's just me and you, Jack."

"Only because I don't want to lose my table; it's in just the right spot to see the ocean, the band, and that table full of girls," I said.

Pat sat down, looked over at the girls, and said, "I thought you and Kaitlyn had something going."

"We do; but that doesn't mean girls aren't nicer to people watch than guys," I said. "So what do you want, and make it quick before you ruin *my* karma."

"I want to know if I can count on your support in the election," said Pat.

"Why do you keep bugging me about that?" I said. "What's so important about me?"

It was true; every time Pat saw me he asked me if I was going to vote for him. It was almost worse than when di islanders were trying to get me to run for the office.

"Because you're the Big Kahuna, Jack," said Pat. "All di islanders respect you; if you endorsed me the election would be over."

"Endorse you? I'm not endorsing anyone," I said. "That would be like endorsing this whole island government thing, which I don't."

"You can't just ignore it," said Pat. "It's going to happen one way or the other."

"Wanna bet? About the ignoring part, that is. Just watch me," I said, while picking up my Chesterita and focusing all my attention on him.

"Maybe here at Chester's grand opening isn't the best time to bring it up," said Pat.

"Not when I've been waiting for a Chesterita for months, and they're finally here to make me feel all warm and fuzzily, no," I said. "That's just a plain bad time for political ads."

"Then we'll talk again, when you're more in the mood for it," said Pat, standing up.

"Good; then wait and find me when I'm dead and buried ten feet under the beach sand. Maybe if I have eternity on my hands I won't mind wasting some of it on frivolous things like politics," I said.

Pat departed, and I tried to get my mind back on all the important things around me. And I did so with the bulk of my gray matter, but a few chunks stayed concentrated on an insidious little thought that had just been put there. A thought that I couldn't quite shake, no matter how much music, Chesteritas, and ambiance it was subjected to. It was obviously something I was going to have to deal with eventually, or I was never gonna have a totally peaceful state of mind.

My own beach bar; hmm...

Chapter Ten
"Oh Won't You Take Them To The Festival."

A week after the festive grand opening of Crazy Chester's, the new Wind Song Resort quietly opened as well, with very little fanfare. The final version of the place had ended up being much smaller than Anderton Corporation's original vision of a huge, sprawling, grand retreat, having evolved into a more intimate fifty room hideaway. Part of that was undoubtedly due to our campaign against the place, but I guessed that not having an airport yet on di island had something to do with it as well.

They did have a fair amount of land to expand on later if they wanted to, of course. And for now, when you booked a room at the resort, it included a one night stay at a property Anderton owned in Puerto Rico, followed by a ride to di island the next morning in a large seaplane that dwarfed Gus's little Noorduyn. I suppose it wasn't the most convenient arrangement, but with the flight into our one particularly tiny harbor it had to be a pretty memorable experience overall.

Pat had finally started leaving me alone about the election, evidently having given up on getting me involved, at least for the time being. He and Wonbago were in fact having trouble keeping any of di islanders very excited about the whole process, and there was a now a general indifference developing to the whole thing. Everyone had been fairly gung-ho about the idea of having a govern-or and a govern-ment at the outset, but it hadn't taken long for it to wear off. Wise people, di islanders.

Coop continued his own campaign, the one for pirate gold, also without my help. He'd been digging holes from one end of di island to the other, but he was still empty handed, except for the single doubloon we'd found together. Although he'd been damned sure he had something big at last when he unearthed a large, wooden chest up on the top of Black Dog's Peak. I thought he was going to cry when he ran to Monkey Drool's looking for help to carry it down the hill, and I had to tell him di islanders and I were the ones who had buried it there in the first place, and that it was only filled with totems from each of us. *Only* to him, of course; they all meant quite a bit to us.

I don't know where Billy had been while Coop was excavating on his turf, but I suspect he was holed up in his cave, choosing to guard it over everywhere else. I know Cooper had made another attempt to get my uncle's permission to search the cavern, bringing a peace offering in the form of a bottle of rum with him. Unfortunately for Coop, the bargaining power of rum with Billy had decreased dramatically over the last couple of years, due to the constant deliveries we made to his cave from the rum factory. It was an example of supply and demand that was good enough to use in any college business course, and for Coop it was yet another setback.

Other than all the openings, elections, and plunder pursuits, life on di island ticked along at its normal pace. Meaning the days all melted into one another, blending together like the ultimate boat drink. It seemed like every time some new thing, place, or human appeared in the mix, di island simply absorbed them into its personality, like someone having a new experience. And like an old friend, it had something new to show and tell you about the next time you visited with it.

As for the Jack that was me, I was of a mind that it was time to shake up my relationship with di island somehow. The song I was currently singing was very melodic and laid back, like a happy, catchy, little tune that gets stuck in your head. But unlike most songs that wedge themselves into your noggin, I never wanted this one to totally go away, no matter how many times I heard it.

At the same time though, I couldn't lose the desire to crank it up a bit for a while, to add a few more notes and make it sound all the richer. Even the best of lives need some days now and then that stand out from the rest, a taste of something different to look forward to and back upon, helping to let you know that time is actually passing. Unfortunately, I didn't have a clue what it was that I felt I was missing.

And then one afternoon it hit me, and in my office of all places. Faith had finally talked me into sitting down and going through some old papers at the rum factory to see if there was anything I wanted to keep before she chucked them all, and I came across the invoice I'd received for the sign for the factory.

I remembered it'd only arrived a day before the factory opened, so the date on the invoice reminded me again exactly when we'd opened our doors. That year we'd thrown a little celebration di islanders called Rum Days, and we did so again on the next couple of our anniversaries as well. But after that it had just faded away for some reason, and other than noticing the date as it went by, we'd done nothing to mark it. And that seemed like a shame to me now; no good reason to celebrate something in life should be left un-toasted, and the opening of the rum factory had changed di island life forever.

So I vowed that this year we'd once again mark the date with a party, then instantly changed my mind and decided it should be a big party, instead. But it wasn't long before it occurred to me that a really big party sounded even better, something that took place all over di island. Maybe even for a couple of days instead of one. And what the hell, why not keep it going for an entire week?

And that's how di island Rum Daze Festival was born. Brazil had Carnival, New Orleans had Mardi Gras, Key West had Fantasy Fest, and the Cayman Islands had Pirate Week. We needed our own festivities to show the rest of the world we could shake our booty with the best of them, something that could grow a little bit every year.

Luckily for my rather short attention span, the next anniversary happened to be in front of us on the calendar as opposed to behind us. If it had just gone by, say two months ago, I probably would have set the whole thing aside as something to do when it grew nearer, and then forgotten all about it again. Instead, it was two months away, a length of time even I could stay focused for, as long as I kept doing things related to it to remind myself it was coming.

There was the teeny tiny problem of trying to throw the whole thing together in just under nine weeks, but I wasn't going to let a little thing like that stop me. I'd thrown parties before at a moment's notice, and now I just had to throw seven of them back to back. Seven parties times a moment's notice to prepare came to only seven moments, so I should have had plenty of time to spare. Then again, I did always suck at math, so maybe my algebraic formula was off.

Luckily for me, yet again, or maybe more so for the festival, my Kaitlyn arrived four days later for three week stay. I'm not sure how much would have gotten done with just me on point, but once she got there and I told her about it, she got excited and organized me. In a lot of ways the festival ended up being as much hers as mine; I came up with ideas for street parties, factory parties, beach parties, and party parties, while Kaitlyn somehow thought up activities during the day that didn't necessarily involve gallons of rum.

Di islanders were more than helpful as well, and it wasn't long before we had all sorts of little things to do all over di island. They embraced the idea of an island festival whole heartedly, and were happy to have a chance to show off the home they were so proud of. Of course, there wouldn't be a whole lot of people to show it off to this first year except for anyone who was going to happen to be visiting in the first place, since nobody was going to know about it ahead of time. But you had to start somewhere, and somewhere was exactly where we were starting.

By the time the opening of the Rum Daze Festival arrived, we were ready to go, more or less. Maybe more and less would be more accurate; while we might have known exactly what we were doing during one given moment, there was a good chance we'd be totally winging it the next. And we didn't really have any kind of set overall theme like we perhaps should have, other than rum, and were instead celebrating every and any little thing that made up life on di island. But I was doing my best not to sweat whether or not it was going to be a success; if people had a good time, then it would be a success, and it didn't matter that we weren't likely to make people change their travels plans any time soon from New Orleans to di island for all their festival needs.

Even *if* ours was gonna be way cooler.

I hoped.

Viva la fiesta!

Chapter Eleven
"Come And Follow In Jack's Wake."

The Crossroads was lined with people one deep as I putted slowly through on my Indian motorcycle. Kaitlyn was riding beside me in the sidecar, tossing beads to people as we went. Both of us were in our finest island attire, I in my favorite Panama hat and rainbow colored tropical shirt with the fuchsia hibiscus, she in her flowered leis, swimsuit, and grass skirt.

My old red bike was decorated as well, covered in garlands. I'd chosen my Indian over my golf cart to be my ride of choice for the parade, which as official Big Kahuna emcee of the festival, I was evidently bound by island law to participate in, or so I'd been told. I felt kind of silly, tooling along and Tour Guide Barbie waving to people, but that's what I got for starting the whole festival thing in the first place.

We were just passing by the Wishing World Fountain that had been built a year back in both the center of the Crossroads and di island. It had been Jolly Roger's idea, as had been the sign asking people to toss coins from their own country into its waters. The coins were collected from time to time, and whenever there were enough, cemented into the seats of the fountain itself, for everyone to see and examine.

And hopefully, refrain from prying out as cheap take home souvenirs.

We'd started our route down at the Wind Song Resort, rolling north by northeast up to the Monkey and Crazy Chester's, then west across di island. It was late afternoon on the fourth day of the festival and the parade was to end at the factory, where tonight's party was set to take place, just down the road from where we'd started.

The first few of days of festivities had been a success, at least by my limbo measuring stick. We'd kicked off with an all day Luau at the Wind Song, which had reminded me of their groundbreaking party a couple of years ago. It hadn't been my first choice for how to begin the festival; the resort was one of the newest parts of di island, and I felt that beginning the whole thing there instead of some place like the factory didn't make much sense. But it had been a good way to get the guests staying there involved at the outset, which had been Kaitlyn's plan all along, and we did need all the people we could get. And Anderton did know how to through a good party, and did so again, I'll give them that.

The next day had been Pirate Day, with that notorious local scallywag and ghost, Captain Billy Black Dog, as the official mascot. I would have tried and tried as hard as I could to get Billy to play himself but I didn't get the chance, since to my surprise, he agreed to do so immediately. Maybe it was because Kaitlyn had asked him; I knew he liked her, as he did most women. And maybe it was because his old friend Moon Man was going to be a pirate as well, albeit a hippified one. But I think what really might have done it was Cooper playing the part of a mean old pirate hunter, whom Black Dog got to push off the southern docks into Mother Ocean. One should never under estimate the seductive powers of revenge.

The highlight of yesterday had been a jerk chicken barbecue and dance at the Sugar Daddy Plantation. My favorite memory of the day was chewing on a few of the raw sugar cane stalks that Ernesto had prepared and handed out to everyone. I'd never tried it before, despite the fact that I'd owned the plantation for a few years now; just goes to show there are always new delights out there in the world to discover and try.

Today I was finding that the biggest drawback to being in a parade, besides carpal-tunnel from all the waving, was not being able to see it. Which was why I was glad I was at the front of it at least. Right behind a float featuring Jedidiah, his steel drums, and all di dancing island kids, pulled by Ernesto and his beloved truck. At least that way I could jump off my bike when we got to the factory, grab a seat, and watch everyone else arrive.

I hadn't been all that keen at first about having a parade as part of the gala, but Kaitlyn had insisted that you couldn't have a decent festival without one. I just wasn't a parade type person, or so I'd thought. I'd never sat down to watch the Macy's Thanksgiving ones on TV as a kid, or any of the cavalcades that went through the Twin Cities during the holidays. I guess I'd never understood them; they hadn't seemed all that exciting to me, but the thing was, they were never really meant to be.

Parades were like baseball, which I'd never really gotten, either. Both were a chance to just sit back and relax, and let the entertainment unfold in front of you at a leisurely pace. And they both had that nostalgic feel to them, a sense of a simpler time. I got all that now; in fact, it was ingrained in my lifestyle. There was nothing more simple than sitting on the beach with a cool drink, wiggling your toes in the sand, and watching the ocean roll in. There were many wonderful, new, exhilarating things to do out in the world today, and they could definitely be a real blast to try. But most of the ones that etched themselves the deepest into your soul were the ones we could have done a thousand years ago. Those were the times when a human was simply being human.

So while maybe I couldn't have ridden my bike in a parade a millennium ago, I certainly could have marched in one. And at the end of my trip around di island, I had to admit that it had been a lot of fun. And it was even more fun watching the other participants roll past the factory and back behind the building; Faith, Cavin, and Captain Billy manning our rum float built mostly of old rum barrels, Michel and Henri on Robichaux's Gumbo Pot trailer, Willie in his rainbow painted island taxi, Crazy Chester's giant papier mache Chesterita, and the Innkeeper riding in my golf cart beside one ugly stuffed sombrero wearing monkey, liberated from the bar for the day to scare small children.

I didn't even mind the campaign politics that our two candidates for governor had brought to the parade; Mr. Wonbago leading the way in his rumbling monster truck with the *huge* tires, and Pat following along behind him, his rotund frame balancing precariously atop one of the tiny mini-motorbikes he sold for kids. I didn't know if one represented big government and the other small, only that the two of them back to back looked damned silly.

But the very best part of the parade? Well, it ended at a rum factory. A rum factory with a patio as decorated as always with brightly colored lights and tiki torches, on a hill above a beach and ocean and my tiki hut. A rum factory who's owner was in charge of throwing the fiesta for this evening.

Luckily, it seemed this guy Jack had enough rum for the night even if a party was involved, so I was happy to humor him and go along with the plan for a while. If I didn't like it, I could always quit and go drink some rum or something.

And as it turned out, I ended up doing both.

Chapter Twelve
"There's The Party."

Parties, as I think I've said before, are living beings. They grow, have personalities, lifespans, and mood swings. And sometimes they can even reproduce.

Our mama party up at the factory had given birth to a baby party down at my tiki shack. A few of us had decided to move there to escape the crush on the patio, getting a bonfire and music going. But it hadn't worked out exactly as I'd planned; our little bambino was growing rapidly as people spotted the fire on the beach and stumbled down the hill to join us. Not that it wasn't still fun, and at least there was more room on the beach to spread out on, but I'd had to put a bench across the door to my shack to block access to non-authorized personnel. Maybe someday they can turn my hut into a Big Kahuna museum if they like and give tours to show where I never grew up, but preferably not tonight while I was still living there.

If I'd had to guess, I would have said that our new party offspring had just passed through its teen years. For a while there it had been acting pretty rebellious while it tried to find its place in the world, and I'd spotted quite a few pimples wandering around. But it had grown out of all that childishness, and was firmly and squarely in its college years. Meaning it was serious and mature about acting like an idiot now.

"I tink you need a bamboo fence, mon," said Roger, looking around at all the party goers.

"It is getting harder to have any kind of private little fiesta down here these days. And ever since the resort opened, people keep wandering through my front yard. But I'd really hate to put up any kind of a wall," I said. "Although I have to admit, I am damned glad right now my tiki bar locks down at least."

"You may have to do someting eventually, though, and der's not much past your place anyway. Di jungle comes right down to di water, and it's hard to walk along di beach after dis," said Roger.

"I don't mind tonight that much, in any case," I said. "This week is supposed to be a party for everyone, and if those everyone want to be here, that's alright by me."

"Dude! Great party, bro!" screamed a fairly thoroughly inebriated merrymaker, having suddenly stuck in his face two inches from mine. Then he whacked me on the back, spilled his drink on my bare feet just before stepping on them, and stumbled away.

"At least I *think* it's alright by me," I said.

"Boss, Cavin wants to know what we should do wit di rum," said Faith, walking up and putting her arm around my waist.

"Drink it," I said, putting mine around her much more slender one.

"I tink he knows dat part," said Faith. "He just wants to know if he should bring some of it down here."

"No, no, no, no, no; that's a really bad idea. We need to at least make people walk back up to the factory if they want a cocktail. If I start feeding all these strays they'll never go home. If any of *you* need anything, just step over the bench and get something from my place; I've got supplies hidden in there," I said. "By the way, where did your trophy go?"

"I locked it in my office at di factory," said Faith. Earlier on, Faith had won the limbo contest we'd held on the factory patio after the parade had ended. "I didn't tink I'd win dis time, wit all dese people."

"I never had any doubt. Watching you limbo is always the highlight of my day; they should make it an Olympic Sport. You'd win the gold, and I'd have a reason to tune in," I said. It was true; seeing Faith do her thing was almost a religious experience, if your religion happened to involve the beauty of the human body and thoughts that would send any conscientious Catholic male running to the nearest confessional. Luckily for me, my religion did embrace all that, along with the rest of the natural and harmless ideas that happily rolled around in my head.

Faith gave me a little squeeze, then let go and said; "Thanks, boss; I better go and tell Cavin to leave di rum right where it is before he starts rolling barrels down di hill."

"Yes, pleazzzz, do that," I said. I watched her go, then turned to Roger. "That Ernesto is a lucky man."

"Ya, dat be true," said Roger. "Faith is a good woman all di way."

"Speaking of good women, I wonder where mine is at?" I said, scanning the crowd while playing *"Where's Kaitlyn?"*

"I tink she went somewhere wit Billy," said Roger.

"You mean, my uncle stole my chick?" I said. "I knew that was going to happen sooner or later; the ladies can never resist dead pirate ghosts."

"She told me a few days ago dat she wanted to get to know him better," said Roger. "I'm sure dat's what she's doing."

"Like I said, they can't resist," I said. I looked myself up and down, suddenly feeling that something was terribly wrong with my picture. "Since you're busy explaining things to me, can you tell me why I don't have a boat drink in my hand?"

"No, dat one I have no idea how to answer," said Roger. "But you better do someting about it before you make di world stop spinning."

"Yes, I better," I said. I made my way through the throng to my tiki hut and stepped up on and over the bench into the inside, and found Gus there, sitting on a chair.

"Hey, Gus. What are you doing in here?" I said.

"Drinking," said Gus.

"I can see that, but why aren't you doing it outside?" I asked, while mixing a rum coke from the makings sitting out on the counter.

"I am doing it outside," said Gus.

"You could have fooled me," I said.

"It's too damned much work climbing over your bench or walking up the hill for every cocktail. So I'm drinking one inside, then mixing another and taking it with me back out there," said Gus. "I'm on the inside part of my rotation right now."

"Would a bigger glass help?" I asked.

"How much bigger?" said Gus, interested.

I opened a cupboard and pulled out the plastic mug I used to make my *"big ass rum and cokes"* and tossed it to Gus. "That should keep you busy for a while; it's about twenty four ounces," I said.

"I guess that'll have to do," grumbled Gus.

"If you want something even bigger I could go hunt down one of the pitchers from under the tiki bar," I said.

"Let me think about it," said Gus.

"Give me back the mug and I'll make you one," I said, holding out my hand.

"No thanks; I'd say you pour like a girl, but that would insult most of the women I hang out with," said Gus, standing up. "Move out of the way and let a man get at the bar."

"Fine; I'll be outside," I said. I clambered back over my bench and banged my shin yet again, then stood in the sand wincing and rubbing it while I observed my surroundings.

What I saw with the clarity that ocean air, rum enhanced blood, and a day filled with fun brings you was a lot of people having a really good time. It was all no problem, mon, and very irie.

And I silently prayed to the tiki gods that it would stay that way for the rest of the night.

Because while all these people on my beach were getting along swimmingly right now, I suddenly realized that if a school of angry sharks showed up and started trouble, there'd really be no one to stop them. I could see now that the scales had tipped and there were just too many strangers visiting di island on a daily basis to keep the status quo'd and that were gonna have to un-quo it soon. When you mixed people together who didn't know each other and filled them with fun but volatile fluids like rum and tequila, their hackles sometimes got raised and their inner cavemen came out. Maybe not with everyone, but sooner or later, someone would puff out their chest and play club the human who'd just bumped into them and spilled their banana daiquiri.

So as much as I hated to admit it, Pat and Mr. Wonbago were right, at least to a point; we did need a little structure on di island, such as a small police force. I hated the idea, though; not that I didn't like and respect the cops back at home. Sure, a few were jerks, but so were some bartenders, and the bartenders didn't have to dodge the occasional bullet (no more so than the rest of us, anyway). What I hated was the fact that we now needed them at all. But then again, maybe having them would mean we wouldn't need them, like nuclear weapons. Or Jedidiah and his tomato stained machete. Or the condom I'd swiped from my father and carried in my wallet all through high school.

Maybe tomorrow I'd go and talk to one of our candidates and see what they had in mind for the future of di island. Or better still, next week. For now I told myself to just relax and have a good time. People were capable of being cool and groovy, and hopefully Moon Man and Mother Ocean's vibes would help keep everyone mellow. But just to make sure, I went over and set my MP3 player to all Bob Marley.

Then I pointed my compass at the nearest fun looking group of people, who happened to be Cavin, Jedidiah, and Ernesto, put up my sails, and tacked on over.

All I needed to light up any dark that might be on the horizon was my good friends, and the only dark I was going to let inside me was my rum.

With the stamina that only years of intensive training can provide, I was able to watch our party reach its elder years. It had grown quite gotten cranky there for a spell, wobbling around unsteadily while complaining how noisy it was and how no one called it anymore. But at last it had come to terms with its old age, and was at peace with itself and the inevitable end of its time on Earth.

I was sitting on a chair next to my fire pit, watching both the dwindling flame and the night sky. The stars, like our party guests, had been vanishing too, giving way to the deep, purplish hues of the earliest signs of morning. Kaitlyn was asleep in my hut, having returned with tales of a successful bonding with my uncle. My only conscious compatriot was a bleary eyed Boyd, who didn't look like he'd be conscious much longer, despite the fact that he didn't himself drink.

"Well, I'd say that was a moderate success," I said.

"People had a good time, that's for sure," agreed Boyd, with a yawn. "Now all you have to do is clean up the mess."

I checked out my beach, which looked like a migrating army of red Solo cup mollusks had skittered through and decided to leave their shells behind. "Yes, that'll be the last mega party on *my* shores. After the festival is over putting up a fence and some private property signs is indeed in order, unfortunately. I'm not about to stop having my little get-togethers with you guys, so I guess I'll have to do something to keep the riffraff out."

"Hopefully that'll work; riffraff herds can be a persistent bunch when they smell fun," said Boyd. Then he yawned yet again, and said, "It's getting late."

"More like getting early," I said. "What's going on again today festival wise?"

"Let's see; it must be Friday. Isn't this *"See di island"* day?" said Boyd.

"That's right; I knew there was a reason it's going to be morning soon and I'm still awake, and it's because I don't have any reason I have to be up in it," I said.

It was true; I had the day completely off, unless I felt like helping out somewhere, which wasn't likely. Jolly Roger was conducting free rides on Mother Ocean circling di island in the Crustacean II, Gus was doing short, ten dollar per person flights to see it from above, while Ernesto was pulling a hay wagon behind the plantation tractor starting at the Crossroads and around di island interior. Plus there was a scavenger hunt that would take its participants from coast to coast to coast to coast. All cool little activities, and all the more so because they had absolutely nothing to do with me being awake before nightfall. Or later.

"So what are you going to do today now that you're free?" asked Boyd.

"Absolutely nothing," I said. "Well, nothing that involves leaving my sandy little piece of property, anyway. Hopefully some quality time with Kaitlyn, as long as she doesn't disappear somewhere again; she's been pretty caught up in all this festival business."

"Having any second thoughts about starting the whole thing up?" said Boyd.

"No, not really," I said. "But you know, if there's one fundamental flaw with we humans it's never being happy with what we have. First I bitch because the resort's being built and more people are going to come to di island, then I decide to organize a yearly festival so even more people will come here in the future. Does that make any sense to you?"

"Sure. It just means you're embracing di new island," said Boyd. "You're good with all the changes, and you're even willing to help them along."

"I am?" I said. "When the hell did that happen?"

Boyd stood up. "I'd say deep down you were probably always okay with it; you just needed time to see that just because di island grows doesn't mean it's not still gonna be di island."

"Well that certainly changes things that I didn't know I'd changed," I said. "But I guess they're good things, aren't they?"

"Yes, they are," said Boyd. "Definitely. But I think it's time for me to go and find my bed, because I can tell you're starting to think too much again, and I don't want to be guilty of helping you do it."

"You're right, I am," I said. "It's my need for rum therapy starting to kick in; happens whenever I stay up too late and it gets really quiet. And I drink a lot of rum, of course. You better get out of here before I try and force you to be my counselor, even though I know deep down I don't need one."

"The first step to recovery *is* admitting that you don't have a problem," said Boyd.

"And that's the tough part," I said. "Because what I keep doing is-"

"What you keep doing is what you're doing right now," said Boyd. "Shut up, stop thinking, and go to bed."

"I will," I said. "But can I just say that-"

"Now!" said Boyd, crossing his arms, and looking down at me sternly.

"Okay, okay," I said. I got up, turned towards my hut and took a step in that direction, then turned back to face Boyd and opened my mouth to say something, then snapped it shut it like a good boy and went inside.

My island head shrinker was right; the last thing I ever needed to do again was ponder my existence. My existence was all pondered out, and if I kept at it much longer I might actually figure it out, and then where would I be? Did anyone really want to know what we were doing here on Earth and what our lives were for? Knowing could turn out to be a helluva lot scarier than being in the dark about it. Either that, or it could turn out to be something so boring and mundane that it would take all the fun out of it. Better to just enjoy the ride and marvel at the mystery of it all.

I knew I'd be happier if I didn't think about my actions and didn't spend so much time trying to figure out their consequences ahead of time. And I'd gotten much better at it, despite my peering down the slippery slope again tonight. I needed to just join Kaitlyn in my hammock and not do anything stupid like wonder why I wanted to, no matter how obvious those reasons appeared to be.

For instance, after I got a little much needed sleep, maybe Kaitlyn and I would participate in some intimate social activities, and maybe we wouldn't. But thinking it over first wouldn't help one way or the other, and nor would it help with most of the things in my life.

Like trying to decide whether or not to kill Cooper when he woke me up a scant two hours later.

Chapter Thirteen
"My Head Hurts, My Feet Stink, And I Don't Love Cooper."

"Pu-lease!" said Cooper.

Coop wasn't begging for his life, although my first impulse had been to make him do just that before exterminating him.

"This is the second time since you've come to di island that you've forced me to be awake before I was ready, and this time I know I didn't tell you to do it," I said.

"Actually, you didn't last time, either," admitted Cooper. "I just made that up. Sorry, mate."

I wondered if it wouldn't be better to do away with him after all, before we did get a police force on di island. "Then why did you tell me I did, and why are you confessing to it now?" I asked.

"Because I needed you to deal with your uncle if we ran into him, but you'd told me the night before I was on my own, so I had to trick you into coming along," said Coop. "And as for 'fessin' up, I couldn't live with the guilt any longer."

"So what the hell do you want this time?" I said, my head and body making several not so veiled threats about severe repercussions if I forced it to stay upright and awake much longer.

"I just told you," said Cooper.

"Well, tell me again, because I wasn't awake before. Not that I'm awake now either, but if you say it enough times it might start to sink in on some unconscious level," I said.

"I want you to come with me treasure hunting again, but this time up to Billy's cave," said Coop. "I need to get in there and look around."

I sighed. "That's not gonna happen; my uncle doesn't want you in there, and that's his right," I said. "It may not look like much, but that cave's his home. I don't think you'd like it if Billy came digging for treasure under the sofa in your living room."

"I don't have a living room; in fact, I don't even have a home," said Coop. "I live wherever I am."

"Then you wouldn't like it if he followed you around and kept digging under your feet," I said. "Besides, is getting in Billy's cave really what you want? Unless it's just to find out about the treasure once and for all?"

"What do you mean? Of course it's about the treasure; I'm here trying to find it, and I do want to know if it's in his cave or not," said Coop.

"In his cave, yeah," I said. "But are you looking for treasure buried by Cofresi, or by Billy?"

"I don't get it," said Cooper.

"Of course you do. You and I have one thing in common, besides both being victims of the Innkeeper's diabolical mixological experiments," I said. "Ever since you dug up that old box at Billy's campsite, we've both been wondering if that single doubloon my uncle put inside it was one of a kind, or if it's one of many Billy has hidden away somewhere, like up in his cave. Perhaps from some long lost pirate treasure he dug up here years ago; a pirate treasure that was originally buried on di island by Captain Cofresi."

"That thought never crossed my mind," said Cooper.

"Yes it did; you even mentioned it at the time. You just don't want to admit it, because if Billy did find Cofresi's treasure and buried it again, that means it belongs to him, now," I said. "Even if you found it once more, you'd be finding Captain Black Dog's plunder, and he's still alive."

"He told me he was a ghost," said Cooper. "But that doesn't matter, anyway. If the treasure's already been found, then so be it. But it should be in a museum if it has."

"Now you're beginning to sound like Indiana Jones," I said.

"Well, Indy had it right," said Cooper. "Look, I just want to see it if nothing else. This is what I do; I hunt for treasure, and treasure the hunt. I'm not trying to get rich. But I would like to know if I was right, and Captain Cofresi did indeed leave some plunder behind here on di island."

"I can understand that," I said. I thought the whole thing over, at least as well as I could in my condition, and came to a decision. "I'll tell you what I'm gonna do, but only if you agree to leave the cave and Billy alone after that. I'll go and talk with him and see if I can find out the truth about the doubloon. It won't be easy; my uncle's not big on truth, especially when his fantasy world is so much more interesting. But I'll do the best I can."

"I guess that'll just have to do, mate," said Coop, obviously a tad disappointed. "But it may not be enough. I mean, even if he says he's found nothing and is telling the truth, Cofresi's swag could be buried right under his nose somewhere in that cave of his and he might not even know it. If that's the case, then neither will we, ever."

"No, we won't, will we? But it's Billy's land. By island law, he owns it," I said. "So know this; I like you, Coop. I really do, in spite of this repeated waking up business. But if I find out later that you've gone up to Billy's cave and trespassed again, I swear I'm gonna have Jedidiah track you through the jungle, boy, and then he'll kick your ass."

"Got it," said Cooper.

"Good," I said. I turned to go back into my shack, then stopped. "Oh, and one more thing; if you ever wake me up again, I'm going to ask Jed to do the same thing, only to bury your body somewhere while he's at it."

I went inside and shut the door, then climbed back into my hammock and snuggled up next to Kaitlyn again.

It's too bad we couldn't solve all di island's present and future problem's by siccing Jedidiah on them. I wished we could just stick to the old ways; one island, under Sol, indivisible by tourists. A place where all mon were created equal, with the right to life, liberty, the pursuit of irie, and island justice for all.

What else could anyone ever really need?

Chapter Fourteen
"This Hidden Cave Got A Lot Of Stuff."

The next evening I walked down the trail from the beached Rum Runner, and up to Black Dog's cave. It was actually the same day that Coop had awakened me, but since I'd gone back to bed I counted it as a new one and tossed the other in the trash, since it's one half hour had had no redeeming qualities.

I figured the cave was where I would find Billy; he'd been pretty scarce over the last month or two, appearing only on special occasions like Pirate Day, when I'd managed to convince him there was a truce in place and his hideout would be safe for the day. That was the main reason I was doing this at all; I would rather have left my uncle alone, but I didn't like the fact he felt he had to stay blockaded in his cave to protect what was his, even if what was his might only turn out to be his S.I. swimsuit issue collection. I wanted the whole treasure thing to be resolved once and for all, no matter how it turned out.

After a little searching I managed to again find the vines that hung down and hid the entrance to his cave, and pushed them aside and entered. I had to give Cooper and/or Cofresi credit; I didn't know if it was a well drawn map or Coop's nose that had led him to find the cavern, but it couldn't have been easy. I shone my flashlight into the darkness, hoping once again that poisonous constricting snakes, vampire bats, giant centipedes, or polar bears with a Caribbean soul hadn't taken up residence with Billy, and went inside.

I managed to take just enough creeping steps into the shadows for it to be as dark as Blackbeard's beard, when Billy decided to leap out and scare any daylight that was left in me out. "Avast, ya scurvy blaggard! Reach for the sky, or I'll run ye through!" he growled.

"There's no sky to reach for, Black Dog," I said, once my heart started beating again. "Just a couple of stalactites. Or stalagmites. Whichever one hangs out up there."

"Jack? Is that you, ya landlubber?" said Billy, peering through the darkness.

I shone the flashlight on my face, temporarily blinding myself even worse than I already had been. "It's me, alright."

Black Dog tucked his cutlass back into his belt. "Ya gotta learn to be more careful, lad; it's not wise sneakin' into a pirate's lair without announcin' yourself first."

"Well, it wouldn't be sneakin' if I did that, now would it?" I said, relieved that Billy seemed to be in a conversational mood at least. "Can I come aboard?"

"Yes, yes; come on in out of the cold, lad," said Black Dog.

"It's about eighty degrees out there," I said.

"Then come on in and get out of the heat," said Black Dog.

I followed Billy to the right, down the passage at the fork in the caverns, the left of which eventually let out into the hidden grotto which you might say was his backyard. It soon grew lighter, and we emerged into the main cave that was his home.

For a hole in a rock, Captain Billy Black Dog's hideout was amazingly cozy. It was lit by old oil lanterns set in indentations in the walls, providing a warm, welcome glow. A hammock hung between two stala-somethings coming out of the ground, next to which sat Sam's bed, currently occupied by Sam himself, who raised his head a bit and wagged his tail at me before plopping back down to snooze. There was an ancient wood burning stove under a hole in the roof that let the smoke out, although Billy usually now cooked out in the grotto on the gas powered Weber I'd purchased for him a few years back. There was enough furniture donated by di islanders scattered about to make the place all the more comfortable, as did the various rugs, paintings and other decorations that festooned the walls, floor, and ceiling. All in all, it was a hideout that would have made Jack Sparrow start molting in envy. And if the other furnishings didn't do it to him, the wine racks filled with bottles of various rums from the factory certainly would have.

"Have a seat, son," said Black Dog, sitting down in his favorite, wooden, high-backed chair, the same one di islanders used to use for their welcome to di island ceremony.

I sat down across from Billy in an old but comfortable rocker, and handed him the basket I'd been carrying. "Here; I brought you some of Akiko's tarts."

Billy opened the basket, looked inside, and took a big, deep whiff. "Mmm; pineapple?" he asked.

"Of course," I said.

"Me favorite," said Black Dog. I knew that, of course. Everyone who liked sweets at all loved Akiko's tarts, and everyone had their own favorite flavor. There was even a list at the general store in the Crossroads, one of the places she delivered to, so you could be sure to buy the right kind for that special friend or someone.

Of course, it was my long lost love, Isabella, who had first baked the fruit filled tarts on di island. But when she'd left for greener Americano pastures, she'd passed the recipe on to Akiko. Akiko had improved on it though, despite the fact that anything Isabella's elegant hands touched had seemed to be better. I know I had been, for those magical months we were together.

Black Dog took out one of the tarts and bit into it, and said, "You're a good lad, Jack, no matter what everyone else tells me. Now what brings ya out on a cold, dark, night such as this?"

At least Billy had the dark part right, and if he wanted it to be cold in his world, who was I to argue with him. "I need to talk to you about Cooper," I said.

"Arr; *that* bilge-sucking addlepate!" grumbled Black Dog. "What about 'im?"

"He's still determined to find Captain Cofresi's treasure," I said. "And I don't think he's going to give up until he finds out once and for all if it's here on di island or not."

"I can't blame 'im for that. It's a pirate's curse that we always be seekin' plunder; even those of us who should be fed to the fish," said Black Dog.

"The thing is, you only whetted his appetite with that single gold doubloon you buried in the box in that clearing," I said.

"What makes ya think it was me?" said Black Dog.

"The note you put inside," I said.

"Oh yeah; forgot about that," said Black Dog.

"Because of that one doubloon, Cooper thinks you may have already found Cofresi's treasure, and hidden it somewhere, like here in your cave," I said.

"And if you did, Coop thinks it should be shown in a museum."

"A pirate's swag in a museum? What kind of loony buccaneer keeps his loot in plain sight for everyone to plunder?" said Black Dog.

I shrugged. "I don't know; someone who wants everyone to be able to see it and lust for it, I guess. It would certainly make the pirate who found it famous, er, notorious," I said. "Just a thought."

"Notorious, eh?" mused Black Dog. "Hmm. So what exactly are ya askin' of me, bucko?"

"I guess I want to know if you did, or not. Find Cofresi's loot, that is," I said.

Captain Billy Black Dog leaned back in his chair and stroked his beard, thinking. Finally he said, "Maybe."

"Maybe? Maybe was the answer before, too; it doesn't tell me much," I said.

"You tell cabin boy Cooper that if he wants me treasure, he's gonna have to earn it," said Black Dog.

"Then you do have it?" I asked.

"Maybe," said Black Dog. "But like I said, he's gonna have to earn it first to find out."

"And just how is he supposed to do that?" I said.

"Like this," said Black Dog, and he leaned forward and began whispering quietly in my ear.

By the time he was finished, I was sure of two things; one, my uncle, dead ghost Captain Billy Black Dog Danielson, was a diabolical rascally naive who I never wanted to cross.

And two, I was glad I wasn't going to be in Coop's shoes and was in my old flip-flops instead.

Chapter Fifteen
"He's A Parrot For The Day."

I don't know about anybody else, but I hate heights, especially high ones. I mean, I really hate 'em. Don't care for them at all. Even if I'd almost jumped off one of the lower cliffs at Rick's Cafe in Negril, which didn't count anyway because it was both alcohol and self esteem fueled. And even then, I still didn't leap, which tells you something right there.

But when I told Roger I thought I would rather have jumped off Black Dog's Peak (if there was a spot you could jump off it) into the ocean instead of being Coop today, I meant every word of it, and I think he agreed with me.

Thanks to Black Dog, we were adding a late entertainment spectacular to the festival. A pirate punishment, of sorts, to be held in the middle of the Crossroads, by the new fountain. A spot where water was readily available, which was a good thing, since there was likely to be some cleanup necessary afterwards.

The kids from di island school had been running around all day with buckets collecting donations, explaining what was going on to the tourists and any islanders who hadn't heard about it already through the Coconut Telegraph. We were hoping to collect at least two thousand dollars, but it didn't really matter since both the Wind Song Resort and Di Island Rum Company had each agreed to donate however much we came up short. The donations had been Faith's idea, once she heard what Black Dog had up his sleeve, and the money was to go to buy a couple of computers for the school. She figured people would be happy to pay to watch the show, so why not feed two parrots with one cracker.

Getting Cooper to agree to it was another matter, especially since Billy still hadn't told me whether or not there actually was a treasure. But I told Coop that if he ever wanted to know, this was the only way to find out. He wasn't happy about it at first, but eventually he managed to get himself into the spirit of the thing, which I'm not sure I could have done.

When the time came, just before sunset, Cooper donned only the pirate hat and pants I'd ordered for him for the festival, and allowed his hands to be tied. Roger and I marched him from inside the 3rd Bank of di island and into the town square, where Black Dog, Sam, and a nice gathering of people waited.

"Hear-ye, hear-ye," said Jolly Roger, the official official at the proceedings. "Captain Coop Bilge Rat Pirate Hunter Walker, ye be charged wit attemptin' to capture a notorious known pirate, Captain Billy Black Dog, in order to stop 'im from plunderin' ships and drinkin' all di rum and becomin' even more notorious. Not to mention ya been tryin' to steal his hard won treasure. How do ya plead?"

"I plead guilty, yer pirateness," said Cooper.

"Let the record show that di blaggard admitted to bein' a low life, black hearted, cur," said Jolly Roger.

"Aye," and "Arr," agreed all the other gathered pirates.

"Since ya never got yer bloomin' mitts on di treasure anyway, and since ya didn't waste even more of our rum drinkin' time arguin' your case, we'll have ta disappoint all these gathered folks and forgo di usual hangin'," said Jolly Roger.

"Booooo," said most of the crowd; evidently tourists were just as bloodthirsty at a hanging as they were at shopping.

"If we're not gonna hang 'im, I demand he at least receive the rum and parrot treatment!" said Black Dog.

"So be it; pirate laddies and lassies, fire away!" shouted Jolly Roger.

I took four big steps back and the hell out of the way, just as Willie, being the oldest, stepped forward and dumped an entire bucket of dark, sweet, and oh so sticky molasses from the sugar plantation over the top of Coop's head. Seconds later, the rest of di island school kids emerged from the crowd, felt pirate hats and red bandanas on their heads, their buckets now filled with colorfully dyed chicken feathers. Soon the area looked like Walt Disney had taken over for old man winter, and had struck the Crossroads with a rainbow blizzard. And when the snowflakes finally cleared, only a prismatic snowman from a land down under remained.

The crowd loved it, and I thought the show was a rousing success and over, but I was wrong. Soon Jedidiah's imposing figure strolled into the square, carrying a very old, familiar, small wooden and metal chest, which he placed on the edge of the fountain. Black Dog walked over to it, and said, "And here be me treasure, for all eyes to see." Then he bent down and lifted back the lid, revealing its contents.

The crowd pushed tentatively forward a bit, a few necks craning to see what was inside. I did so as well, because even though I already had a good view, I didn't know exactly what I was looking at.

I don't think anyone else did, either. Yes, it was shiny. And yes, it was yellow. Neither of which meant it was real. But then the waning sun peaked through the buildings and people at just the right angle, bouncing off the contents of the chest and making it glitter in that way that nothing on Earth but gold does.

I'm sure most of the audience probably assumed it was fake; I mean, how many times do you see a chest full of gold coins just sitting there in front of you, no matter how small it was? But I knew right away they were real, perhaps because I'd already seen the one doubloon. And I knew the rum parrot standing next to me attracting flies knew as well.

I looked over at him, his eyes peaking through his feathered facade. He was just staring down at the gold, and I couldn't help wondering if any of the hundreds of photos that had been and were still being taken of the event would make it into the museum next to the doubloons. It would be one helluva way to be immortalized.

"Well, there it is," I said to Coop.

"I know; I can't believe it," said Cooper.

"Have you ever found any treasure before?" I asked.

"Yes, but not like this; just bits and pieces, single items and such," said Coop. "But then, I didn't find this one, either."

"Billy said he wants to share di credit wit you," said Roger, coming up behind us.

"He does?" said Cooper, finally turning away from the gold to look at Roger.

"Yeah; he doesn't care. He wants his name on it with yours, and he wants di money for it, but he said you can say you two found it together," said Roger. "Which in a way is true."

"Where did he find it?" asked Cooper.

"In the cave, like you thought," said Roger.

"So you knew about this?" I said. "About the treasure?"

"Yeah, mon," said Roger.

"For how long?" I asked.

"Oh, about two years; that's when I helped him bury di box in di clearing," said Roger. "Of course, I thought all di doubloons were in it at di time, and not just one, but I guess he only trusted me so far. I don't know where he had di real treasure hidden all dis time."

"Two years and you never said anything?" I said.

"Nope; you be lookin' at di only islander who can keep a secret," said Roger, smiling. "Anyway, Billy found di gold when he was lookin' for a spot for his pirate throne. He had a place he wanted to put it, right by dat broken off stalagmite he uses as an end table. But there was a rock in di way, and when he moved it, he found di box underneath."

"That figures; a lot of treasure gets found by accident," said Coop, blowing a loose feather away from his beak, er, mouth.

"Billy said you do have to say you two found it in dat clearing on your map," said Roger. "He doesn't want anyone else snooping around in his cavern."

"Fine by me," said Cooper. "I'm grateful he's letting me have any credit at all."

We stood looking at the gold for a moment or two longer, then I said, "So was it worth it?"

"Are you asking me?" said Cooper.

"No, I'm asking Big Bird," I said. "Of course I mean you. The whole thing; the hunt, the wait, the threats, and now," I gestured up and down at him, "all this. Are you happy, now?"

Coop smiled a big, broad smile, unmistakable in spite of his plumage. "Too right, mate! It's pretty damn spiffy; real bonzer! Ripper, you know?"

I didn't know, but I could tell Coop was feeling colorful again.

And this time he looked it, too.

Chapter Sixteen
"I've Got A Question For You."

I was nibblin' on crab cake, and watching the sun bake all of these very tired tourists.

It was late afternoon the last day of the festival, and everyone was pretty tuckered out, including me. I'd already made a note to myself that perhaps Rum Daze would be a better event if it was shorter, say four much more manageable days. I didn't see any reason why we had to go the full seven just because some guy in a toga had decided that's how many days were in a week; how the hell did he know, anyway? For all he knew there were only six. Or five. Or like our festival would show if I had any say in the matter, four.

Today we were having an island food and craft fair on the eastern beach between Crazy Chester's and Robichaux's. It reminded me a little of being back on Mallory Square in Key West, except there was sand under my soles instead of stone and brick. And we were on the wrong side of di island to watch for the green flash at sunset.

But while we'd be missing Sol's last glorious rays as he sank into Mother Ocean, we were making up for it nicely with our food selection. So far I'd sampled gumbo, blackened mahi-mahi, conch fritters, breadfruit pie, coconut curry pumpkin soup, papaya salad, Caribbean spiced nuts, and jerk chicken pizza. And Jack, there was still so much to be done. And digested.

"Here you go," said Kaitlyn, handing me a cup of mango iced tea before sitting down next to me on our blanket in the sand. I'd been literally too stuffed to move, and in need of some lubricant to make room for more goodies.

"Thanks," I said, taking a sip. I managed to refrain from gulping it all down at once, something I had difficulty doing with many of the beverages on di island, alcoholic or not. There was just something about the drinks here; maybe it was the heat or the ocean air that made everything taste better. Or maybe they went down quicker because so many of them weren't carbonated. Then again, maybe mango, key lime, papaya, banana, kiwi, pineapple, and coconut were just plain tastier than carbonated water, caffeine, high-fructose corn syrup, and phosphoric acid v caramel.

Whatever the reason, my mango tea refreshed me as always, and I was able to consider my next move, which turned out to be a quick kiss on Kaitlyn's cheek. Along with a big chunk of the tourists, she was leaving tomorrow, and I was trying to squeeze in as much we time as possible.

It felt like I was going to miss her more this departure than usual, probably due to our island party ending at the same time. Although our festival had drained me and I was glad in a way it was coming to an end, it was a melancholy gladness. The whole thing had been a lot of fun, like a great vacation, and like a vacation I was both happy and sad it was over. And that mixed feeling was spilling over onto Kaitlyn; not that I was ever happy to see her go, but this time it seemed, well, just more.

"When are you coming back?" I asked.

"I'm afraid it might be a while this time," said Kaitlyn, between bites of coconut sweet bread. "Anderton is looking to expand somewhere around Australia and New Zealand, so I'm going to be a little too far away to pop in for a weekend visit."

"How long is a while?" I asked, already dreading the answer.

"Probably about a month," said Kaitlyn.

"A month!?" I exclaimed. "I don't think I can live without you for that long."

"Yes, you can," said Kaitlyn.

"No, I can't," I said. "I mean, look around; the ocean keeps rolling gently in and out, in and out, in and out, passionately caressing the sand, and then one thing leads to another, and..."

"Maybe you should stay inland, then," said Kaitlyn.

"Well, setting aside the fact that I live on the beach, even if I go inland, then I get supple palm trees swaying to and fro in the hot, steamy, tropical breeze," I said.

"Don't you see palm trees on the beach, too?" asked Kaitlyn. "And since when are they supple?"

"They become supple whenever you're gone," I said. "And I don't notice them on the beach because I'm too busy watching the ocean go in and out, in and out, in and out..."

"You do have problems, don't you?" said Kaitlyn.

"You have no idea," I said.

"So what are we going to do about it?" said Kaitlyn.

"Let's get married," I said. It was something I'd like to pretend I'd just said without thinking of the consequences, but the truth of the matter was I'd been considering it all week. "Tonight."

"Jack..." said Kaitlyn.

"Is that a yes, Jack, or a no, Jack," I said.

"It's a no, Jack," said Kaitlyn.

"Why not?" I asked.

"First of all, because it wouldn't change anything, at least not my leaving, which is why you asked me in the first place," said Kaitlyn.

"That's not why I asked you," I said.

Kaitlyn gave me one of *those* looks.

"Okay, it was, but that was only part of the reason," I said. "I've been thinking a lot about it, and I just plain want to marry you."

"And you will," said Kaitlyn.

"When?" I said.

"How about a year and one week from today?" said Kaitlyn.

I hadn't expected any kind of firm answer, let alone one so precise, and it took me more than a little by surprise. "Really? Are you sure?" I said.

"Yeah; yeah, I am," said Kaitlyn. "I've been thinking about it, too; about everything. And I've decided to give my job one last year, and then call it quits and move to di island for good. I figure I'll be unemployed by the time next year's festival starts, and a week after it ends we can get married."

"Wow; you know, I didn't really think you'd say yes," I said.

"Well, don't point a marriage at someone if you don't plan to use it," said Kaitlyn.

"Oh, I plan on using it, believe me," I said. I was a bit in shock, in a good way, and not sure how to react. "Do you want to kiss or something?"

"Naw; maybe later," said my sudden fiancè. "But I would like to go get one of Akiko's key lime tarts."

"Then let's go," I said, standing up. "But I'm getting mine papaya."

We walked hand in hand through the sand to Akiko and Crazy Chester's stand, everything seeming even more lyrical than before. It had come about so simply, like all of the best things in my life, and just as out of the ocean blue; I was engaged.

It looked like from now on my song would always be a duet.

Chapter Seventeen
"The Night We Painted The Sky."

The nighttime sky over di island's eastern ocean was a rainbow of sparkling hues, thousands of shooting and falling stars painting an iridescent brushstroke across Earth's stratospheric canvas. That's how I saw the fireworks, anyway, through the eyes of someone who was feeling like he was up there with them, and more than a little bit giddy. Someone, meaning me.

Kaitlyn and I were still cuddled on our blanket in the sand, except the phrase *"Kaitlyn and I"* didn't feel like it summed us up well enough anymore. It seemed to me we should have a new title, and not the standard mister and misses prefixes we would eventually be dubbed with. Something like *"Kaitack"* or *"Jacklyn"*, neither of which did much for me. Although I was sort of fond of *"Kait'n'jack"* which sounded like a name for something piratey.

An alternate moniker might have made my new fiancè happy as well; although she said she didn't mind, she'd couldn't help but point out that the name Kaitlyn Danielson bordered on being a tongue twister. I told her I'd happily become Jack Mars, instead, which sounded like the name of a dashing and daring rocketeer in a forties movie serial. But she said she wanted to be traditional, so I was stuck being a sour mash maker's son.

Our fireworks display marked the official end of di island Rum Daze Festival. When I'd been doing my research on other festivals it seemed like their fireworks were always near the beginning of their fiestas, but I felt they should be at the end, a sort of grand finale to just sit back and relax to after a long week of revelry. I kind of figured they'd be a welcome respite, especially if you were leaving and flying home early the next morning. I know they certainly felt just right to me.

Obviously our humble little spectacle wasn't putting Disney World's twenty-eight hundred shells per night show to shame, but we had our moments, all things considered. And ours was over Mother Ocean, which did it no end of good aesthetics wise.

A cannon shot from Black Dog's Peak had signaled the start of the show, fired off by Willie. I wasn't sure about letting a just turned sixteen year old man the guns, but things were different on di island. And if Black Dog himself trusted Willie to play bombardier, something he'd never allow me to do, even if I had the guts to go near the thing while it went bang, then I guessed I could trust him, too.

As for Black Dog himself, the reason he wasn't personally handling Lady Boomer was because he was out on di Isla De Luis being Moon Man's assistant. Di Isla De Luis was a small piece of land sticking out of the ocean about a quarter mile off the shore of di island. We didn't know if it had an official handle on any of the maps or not; it was only about a football field across at high tide. But Cavin had decided to name it after Luis, our wise, good friend and Cavin's mentor at the rum factory, who'd passed into the great beyond a few years ago. And the rest of us couldn't agree more with his memorial.

For this evening, di Isla De Luis was being used as our Cape Canaveral for the fireworks launchings. Luckily for us, Moon Man was turning out to be a bit of a renaissance Luna man; his hands had tried many things throughout his life, and one of those hands had fiddled around with being a pyrotechnician. So he and Billy were out on the near horizon, playing pirate astronauts for the night. I wished I could see Billy's face; there wouldn't be many things in life that would put a bigger smile on his puss than firing rocket after rocket into the Southern Cross's domain.

As another explosion of light blossomed above, and another chorus of oohs and aahs rolled over the beach like a gentle surf, I couldn't imagine a more perfect day, a more perfect way to end the festival, or a more perfect way to spend what was to be my last night with Kaitlyn for some time. Of course, there were a few other things I was hoping to do later with Kaitlyn as well, but doing them on a beach filled with people didn't seem entirely proper, even somewhere as laid back as di island.

So I decided to skip the after fireworks party at Crazy Chester's, in favor of performing my own pyrotechnic show with my fiancè in my tiki shack instead.

Ooh, and aah.

Chapter Eighteen
"We Got A Lot We Should be Drinking About."

A few days later I'd said my goodbyes to Kaitlyn and Coop. Both were temporary; hopefully I'd see the love of my life in about a month or so, and Cooper had promised to return to di island for a visit after he found a home for Cofresi and Black Dog's plunder.

I didn't know what to expect from the treasure, which had three hundred and forty-two coins total. There would have been three hundred and forty-six, but Billy took one and gave one each to myself, Cooper, and Jolly Roger for us to keep. I was of a mind to carry mine around in my pocket for good luck, until Black Dog reminded me I was an idiot and would lose it within a day, therefore giving me bad luck forever. So I put it in a safe place in my office at the factory instead, under Billy's stuffed baby alligator, until I got around to getting a fancy glass display case and satin pillow for it.

As for Kaitlyn, I missed her immediately this parting. Not that I didn't always miss her to some degree, but usually it took a while before it started gnawing at me. There was something about being engaged that seemed to make her absence harder to deal with, as if we were more connected now; I tried to tell myself that we we'd always been connected and there was just a promise in place now and to man up, but I was never a very good listener when it came to me own advice.

At least I had a distraction coming in a few days; it was time for one of my old friend Marty's random visits to di island, something I was greatly looking forward to. I wished at first that Kaitlyn was going to be here so Marty and his wife could both spend some time with the better half shell of my oyster of love (Moon Man's words, not mine), but Marty was flying solo himself this trip, anyway. So it looked like it was meant to be a boy's weekend out.

Marty and Bonnie had been doing well since they'd grabbed the kids and migrated down to Naples, Florida, from my own old stomping grounds, Mini Soda. And better still (especially Marty) once they'd shifted their nest up the coast a bit to Sanibel, putting at least a little distance between themselves and Bonnie's parents. Marty came to di island about twice a year now, usually bringing the rest of the family on every other trip or so.

The fact that he'd be coming alone fit nicely into a new hair brained scheme I was hatching and working on, but at the moment there were other less important and definitely more nefarious things to deal with on di island. And though I'd tried to avoid all contact with it as if it were the plague, there were too many other people who'd already been infected to stay entirely electionitis free.

You could say that the whole thing was coming to a head now, and that people were really into the whole political process. You *could* say that; what would be more accurate would be to say that people were putting up with it, and that the battle between Pat and Wonbago was coming to a head. Meaning, the two of them were arguing every chance they got, while everyone else just sat back and watched with a detached and bemused disinterest.

Roger, though, had decided that something had to be done if we were going to do this thing at all, something to apply some kind of organization to the whole mess. Mr. Wonbago had at least scheduled an election date, since he was the only thing close to a public official di island had at the moment. But what Roger wanted, and finally was to get this evening, was a town hall meeting.

I wanted to call it an island bar meeting, since it sounded like more fun and was being held on Crazy Chester's rooftop, but I got voted down, proof to me we didn't need actual government to have democracy. In any case, the idea was to get any and every one who cared at all into one spot, along with Pat and Wonbago, and I suppose, grill the hell out of the two of them. I was always willing to try something new, but I wasn't sure blackened or jerked candidate was going to sit well with my palette.

When the hour of the big event finally came, I almost hoped I'd find no one up top as I ascended Chester's stairs. But to my surprise, the roof was almost full; evidently the general apathy over the whole election was no match for di islanders love of gathering together for whatever the reason. Pat and Wonbago were sitting on bar stools up on the stage, and between them stood Roger, who'd agreed to play moderator (I'd voted for Jedidiah and his machete, but Roger was a solid second choice). I took a seat next to Ernesto and Faith, and waited for the circus act to begin.

Roger cleared his throat. "I guess we can get started; you all know why we're here. Who wants to ask di first question?" he said, diving right into the waters.

Gus raised his hand, then stood up and said, "Isn't anyone gonna serve drinks?"

"Afterwards," said Roger. "Dis is an official election proceeding, so no alcohol."

"I know it's an official election proceeding; that's why I need a drink," said Gus. "And if you think there's no alcohol in politics, go to D.C.; it's one big cocktail party."

"Well, not here," said Roger. "We start dat and dis will turn into one big party, too."

"Heaven forbid," said Gus, and he sat back down.

"I have a question," said Boyd.

"It's not about food, is it?" asked Roger.

"No," said Boyd. "Although that wouldn't be bad, either. I want to know why Mr. Wonbago thinks he needs such a big, gas-guzzling, noisy, truck."

"Does dat have someting to do with being di governor?" asked Wonbago.

"Yeah, of course it does; how do we know you'll look after di island if you're rumbling and polluting all over it right now?" said Boyd.

"My truck doesn't pollute any more den Ernesto's pick-up," argued Wonbago.

"But he's not running for governor," said Boyd.

"He should be," said Faith. "He'd be better den you two."

"Thanks, sweetie," said Ernesto.

"You're welcome, honey," said Faith.

"Can we get back to di election business?" said Roger. "How do you answer, Mr. Wonbago?"

Wonbago shrugged, and said. "We have di roads. I have di truck. I don't see any reason not to put di one on top of di other."

"Next question," said Roger.

"I'd like to point out that the only vehicles I ride are my little energy efficient scooters," said Pat.

"Who asked you, mon?" said Wonbago.

"That's the way this works," said Pat. "We all get to talk."

"Well den, I want to say dat maybe one of your scooters doesn't pollute much, but you rent out a bunch of dem every day, so together dey be makin' quite a mess, I bet," said Wonbago.

"That's different," said Pat.

"Look, we've talked about dis one question long enough; if we keep goin' like dis it's gonna take all night," said Roger.

"And then I'm definitely gonna need a drink," grumbled Gus.

"Right, so let's move on before Gus gets any crankier," said Roger. "Who's next?"

"Me," said the Innkeeper. I was surprised to see him there, which meant that Monkey Drool's was closed, and Francis didn't like to lose any chance to make a dollar. Evidently the election was important to him for some reason.

"Go ahead," said Roger.

Francis stood up, and unrolled a large piece of paper he was carrying. "I have a map of some new zoning areas I tink would help keep di island di way it was meant to be, and I was wondering which candidate would approve dem."

"Let me see that," said Chester, getting up and going over to examine the drawing. "Hey, you've got the commercial zone on this beach penciled in so it ends right down the middle of my property!"

"Yah, dat be too bad, I know. But my study shows dat it would be better dat way," said the Innkeeper.

"For who?" demanded Chester.

"It would be wrong if it was better for just one person, so I can't say; luckily dis is just better better," said Francis. "You know, in general."

"And what would happen to my bar?" said Chester.

"I been tinkin' about dat; it would be tough for me, but I could buy di half of your land dats next to mine," said the Innkeeper. "And after you tear di building down I could take di wood off your hands so you don't have to haul it away."

"That's mighty nice of you!" fumed Chester.

"Ya, mon; I know. Lucky for you, I been tinkin' of expanding," said Francis.

"What a coincidence," said Chester.

"So which one of you two would vote yes on dis?" said Francis.

"I would have to take a closer look at it and do a study to see what was best for everyone," said Pat.

"I told you; I already took di closer look and did di study," said the Innkeeper.

"Still," said Pat. "We'd need an independent study."

"I might be willing to make di change," said Wonbago.

"Den I'm voting for you, mon!" said Francis.

"And I'm not!" said Chester.

"Dat be up to you," said Francis. He rolled up his map and said, "I gotta go back to work; I heard everyting I want to hear. Two for one drinks at di Monkey while di election meeting is going on!"

"And after that?" said Gus.

"Full price, of course," said the Innkeeper.

"Then I'm going with you now; I've heard everything I didn't want to hear, too," said Gus, and the two disappeared down the stairs.

"Well, dats probably for di best," said Roger. "Who else has a question?"

"I do," said Ernesto. "What about about the airport?"

"Dat's already settled," said Wonbago. "By me, so it just shows I can get di job done."

"Yes, but too quickly; did you even look at the consequences of where you put it?" said Pat. "There should have been a study."

It was true; the land for the airport had been suddenly designated out of the blue, so to speak. Anderton was helping with the construction costs, and di island would gradually be paying them back. Just another necessary evil, I guess. Although evil or not, it was going to be nice to again be able to fly to one of the other places my song sang, like Key West or New Orleans.

"So was dat your question, Ernesto?" asked Roger.

"No; I jus wanted to know eef there was going to be a freight building at the airport, to ship out the rum, sugar, and other things we make on di island," said Ernesto.

I would have chastised me for not asking that question myself, and a long time ago, but me and I both knew Ernesto had a lot more common sense than we did, so we weren't all that surprised that he'd beaten us to it.

"Ya, mon; I tink we could do dat," said Mr. Wonbago.

"I agree with my esteemed colleague this time, but we should conduct a study first to make sure it's done properly," said Pat.

"Gracias," said Ernesto.

"Finally," said Roger. "Maybe we be on di right track now. Who's next?"

Nobody said anything for a moment, so I decided now was as good a time as any to get it over with, and I raised my hand meekly.

"Jack, you have a question, mon?" asked Roger.

"Actually, it's a question from Billy, er, Captain Black Dog. He wrote it down for me, and I have it here, somewhere," I said, digging through my pockets. "I haven't looked at it yet; I've been a bit afraid to."

"We can take it," said Faith.

I found the paper and unfolded it, quickly read through it to make sure I could repeat it in public, and said, "It's a two part question."

"What's di first part?" asked Roger.

I read the paper aloud, in my best Black Dog voice. "Avast, ye! For kidnappin' and ransomin' the governor purposes, I was wonderin' which one of ya two blaggards is wealthier. And if either of ye has a lovely daughter I don't know about, for the same reason."

Nobody said anything at first, so Roger said, "Well?"

"I'm barely getting by," said Pat.

"All my money is tied up in offshore stocks and bonds," said Mr. Wonbago.

158

"And di daughter?" asked Roger.

"I have one, and she is lovely, but she's nine and back in Canada with my ex-wife," said Pat.

"And you, Mr. Wonbago?" said Roger.

"No comment," said Wonbago.

"What's di second part of Billy's question?" said Roger.

"Oh," I said, trying to guess what Wonbago's no comment meant. "Basically Billy wants to know what's going to be done about all the tourists playing on the Rum Runner; a couple of them have even carved their names on it. But actually, I can answer this, myself. I've already decided to move it down to the beach in front of my hut, as soon as Jedidiah and Willie are done with the wall they're putting up around my property. That way he'll be closer and I can keep an eye on it," I said. "That is, if I can go ahead and do it without conducting a study, first."

"Very funny," said Pat, sourly.

"I tink I can approve dat for you," said Mr. Wonbago.

"Good. Next question?" said Roger.

The rest of the evening pretty much went the same way. There were a couple of borderline major concerns that came up, a whole lot of minor ones, and a very heated debate that broke out over whether or not we needed to designate an official national fish to go with the new national anthem, flag, flower, tree, and bird we were working on adopting. When the meeting finally came to a close around midnight, I wished I'd been at Monkey Drool's with Gus the whole time, instead.

But there was nothing to stop me from spending the next couple of hours making up for lost time.

Chapter Nineteen
"Trying To Reason With Political Season."

One Pickled Parrot, two Toasted Toucans, and three Cockeyed Cockatoos later, I was finally feeling cleansed enough to bring up the subject of our political debacle to my own group of esteemed colleagues. "So; what did you guys think of our candidates?" I said.

"I tink we be in big trouble, mon," said Roger.

"No shit, Sherlock," said Gus. "I could have told you that a long time ago."

"I don't know; I'll have to do a study about it first, and then get back to you," said Boyd.

"I just know I don't want to vote for either one of them," said Cavin. "I mean, I like Pat, and even Mr. Wonbago, just for being Wonbago, but I don't think either of them should be in charge."

"Agreed," I said. "But we do need to get some rules in place, and some support structure. We just have too much contact with the rest of the world, now."

"I say we destroy the docks and burn down the resort and rum factory," said Gus.

"We went through all that when the resort was opening," said Cavin. "We can't do it again."

"No, there be no turning back di clocks, now," said Roger. "And dat's okay."

"Then lets just do a write in and elect the Big Kahuna here, whether he likes it or not," said Boyd.

"I'm not being governor, and that's final," I said. "Unless you can find a way to make it as glamorous as it was in Pirates of the Caribbean and Captain Blood."

"If we do, you have to wear the powdered wig," said Boyd.

"Never mind," I said. "And come to think about it, governors usually just get abused in pirate movies."

"Then what do you genius's think we should do?" said Gus.

"I've got an idea," said Willie, who'd been sitting quietly listening to everyone else. "Although I don't know if it's something we could do or not."

"Spill it," said Gus. "I'd consider anything at this point, no matter how crazy."

Willie paused, as if he wasn't sure what he had to say was worth saying, then said, "I just thought maybe we could have an island council instead of a governor."

"An island council?" said Boyd.

"Yeah; Mr. Wonbago does things too quickly and spontaneously, and would do anything to be in charge. And Pat thinks so much before he does something that it takes forever to get it done," said Willie.

"Like thinking about renting out dive equipment at his store for two years running?" I said.

"Exactly," said Willie. "He just seems like he'd be a typical bureaucrat if he was our governor."

"So what are you suggesting, exactly?" said Cavin.

"Why don't we put both of them on a council?" said Willie.

"You mean, since we don't want either of dem, elect both of dem, instead?" said Roger.

"Well, yeah," said Willie.

"It makes sense, actually," I said. "That's what we do back in the states, except we call them senators and congressmen."

"At least they'd keep each other in check," said Boyd. "But two people on a committee isn't a good idea; too many deadlocks. We'd need one more person."

"Don't look at me," I said, when everyone turned and did just that.

"Who, then?" said Gus.

"I'll do it," said Roger.

"You will?" I said, surprised, since Roger had shown no interest when I'd asked him to run so I could have someone worth voting for.

"Yeah," said Roger. "I don't mind helping di island become a better place; I just didn't want to be in charge of it all."

"The perfect candidate; someone who wants to help but doesn't want to be in power. What the hell planet are you from, anyway?" said Gus.

"It works for me; all in favor say aye," I said, before Roger could change his mind.

"Aye," said everyone at the table.

"Nice going, Willie," said Gus.

"Thanks," said Willie, looking happy.

"And as a reward, you get to tell Wonbago and Pat all about how neither of them is going to get to be governor," said Gus.

"Damn; I was hoping to get to do that," said Cavin.

"Do you think they'll go for it?" said Boyd.

"They won't have any choice," I said. "They both wanted me to endorse them, so now I'm going to go around and do just that, along with Jolly Roger here and the whole idea of an island council."

"Nothing like wielding power in a bar," said Gus. "I told everyone we should have had drinks; just look how good they worked."

"In rum we trust," said Cavin.

Maybe someday we could elect a governor to sit above the council, but I didn't think the island was ready for it, or needed one, quite yet. Three heads would work better than one, especially since one of those heads was now going to be Jolly Roger's.

It looked like the pirate party had come to power at last.

Chapter Twenty
"Please Bypass This Brain."

Pat and Mr. Wonbago were none too pleased at first, especially Wonbago, about our nonviolent overthrow of the government that wasn't even governing yet, but eventually they got over it. Part of it was probably because they still were going to get to wield power, and didn't even have to worry about getting elected. And the other part was that they didn't have any choice in the matter; the nicest thing about not having a bureaucracy yet was that anyone could pretty much do whatever they wanted, as long as nobody else cared. And nobody on di island gave a pair of fetid goat's kidneys that we were going to have an island council instead of an island governor, especially since it put an abrupt halt to any and everything campaign related.

The council was set to take power the same day as the election was previously going to be held, which meant our little rum powered coup d'état was likely to be the last such government free rules decision di island would ever experience. From that point on, the council would deliberate and make a decision on just about everything on di island. Including a referendum for a recurring election to vote in a new council to begin in a few years, which Pat said would be their first act.

My police would be coming soon as well, but after the council made a few laws so they'd have something to actually enforce. So until the first ticket for jay walking across a goat path could officially be issued, we'd have to make do with having Jedidiah on call.

My own little part of the world had already become a little more protected from the rest, or at least more privatized. The fence around my property was now finished; it was tall and made of bamboo and wood along the back and part of the side, turning into a low stone number as it approached the ocean so I could still see down the beach. My private property signs were up as well, but since I didn't own a parrot yet, I refrained from any *"protected by attack bird"* postings. I knew I'd still have the occasional unannounced visitor trampling through my sea shells, but hopefully it would thin their numbers a bit.

Billy's old and broken Rum Runner had been moved all the way across di island from its long beached spot near Monkey Drool's, and placed in the same position on my own beach. I hadn't been sure at first if Black Dog would go along with it or not; the old site was where his ship had washed up on shore, so I figured it had to have some meaning to him. But he

surprised me by saying it was time for he and the Rum
Runner to move on, and placing it in a harbor safe
from the tourists was more important to him. He also
said that he was even willing to put up with seeing
more of me, too, which he knew he would once he was
anchored in my front yard. As always, it felt good to be
loved.

But the biggest event, to me anyway, was
Marty's arrival on di island this morning. He was going
to be staying at my place this time, as opposed to the
plantation house, where Jedidiah now lived. I had
plenty of sleeping spots so we wouldn't have to cozy
up to one another; one hammock inside and one out, as
well as a comfortable sleeping mat in the bedroom.
Not that I planned on us being there much.

I met Marty down at the southern docks as he
disembarked from Gus's seaplane, then we took a ride
up to Crazy Chester's in my golf cart. Soon we were
munching island goodies from one of Chester's
appetizer samplers, and sipping cold Chesteritas as we
caught up on eachother's lives.

"Engaged?!" exclaimed Marty.

"You sound surprised," I said.

"Yeah, I am," said Marty. "I figured you'd end
up thinking another relationship to death, like you did
with Isabella."

"Now you sound like Billy," I said.

"Well, Isabella was the best thing that ever happened to you or any man on Earth, and you let her get away by waiting too long to reel her in and mount her on the wall," said Marty.

"I'm not going to touch that wall line," I said. "Anyway, Isabella fought too hard; I'm not exactly the Old Man and the Sea when it comes to fishing for women, you know. Besides, Kaitlyn is the best thing to ever happen to me, too, so I got to have it happen to me twice."

"They can't both be the best," said Marty.

"I've learned they can. Just like two beaches; it just depends on which one you're laying on at the moment," I said.

"Now who's the one spouting innuendos?" said Marty.

I grabbed a coconut crab bite and popped it into my mouth. "Besides, I never thought much about Kaitlyn's and my relationship; I'm out of the deep thinking business for good. I only use a few light thoughts now and then to keep my bodily functions going," I said.

"Then you don't think when you talk?" said Marty.

"I do, but talking is a bodily function, too," I said. "Like breathing."

"Yeah, you're probably right about that. Try getting people to shut up for two minutes; even when they're finally alone in their cars and could enjoy some peace and quiet for a change, they instantly call someone," said Marty. "Cellphones must be a kind of vocal oxygen tank."

"The main thing I'm not using my thought for anymore though is to make decisions," I said.

"How do you decide something, then?" asked Marty.

"I just go with whatever sounds best," I said. "I'm kind of on impulse mode; you should try it."

"So really, you're like a little kid; you see something you like and just stick it in your mouth," said Marty.

"Kind of, yeah," I said, seeing a conch fritter and sticking it in my mouth. "Think about it."

"You just told me not to," said Marty.

I thought about that, something I just said I didn't do anymore. "Let me put it a different way," I said.

"You want me to forget everything you just said, then?" said Marty.

"No, keep it in mind as a reference, but I'm rebooting the conversation," I said.

"Gotcha," said Marty. Marty and I used to have discussions like this all the time when we'd worked together at Image Makers back in Minnesota. They kept us sane, no matter how insane they actually sounded.

"What part of our lives are we really the happiest in?" I asked.

"Probably when we're getting lucky," said Marty.

"I meant, what age are we the happiest in?" I said. "It's when we're kids, right?"

"I don't know about that," said Marty.

"Sure it is. And it's because we just enjoy whatever we're doing without giving it a lot of thought, like questioning whether we should be doing it or not, or what someone else might think about us because of it," I said. "We're just doing it for the sheer joy of it, whatever it is, and living in the moment."

"Like getting lucky," said Marty.

"No, we usually think about that one, too; a lot, actually, before *and* after," I said.

"That still leaves the during for no thinking, which is what you were saying to begin with," said Marty.

"Fine, if you insist; we're happiest when we're kids, *and* when we're getting lucky," I said.

"So what you're basically saying is we should all not worry about things and just go for it?" said

Marty. "Not exactly Earth shatteringly new advice, Jack; I expected better from you."

"No, I know. And it's not even close to what I meant," I said.

"Then what did you mean?" said Marty.

I looked around Crazy Chester's rooftop at all the seemingly happy faces; everyone looked like they were having a good time. And me?

"Do you remember that dinner back in Minneapolis when I was holed up at the Ramada Inn after the crash?" I said.

"How can I forget?" said Marty. "You told me over chicken enchiladas that you were going to live your life like a Jimmy Buffett Song; that sort of loony proclamation from your best friend tends to stick in your memory."

"I also told you I didn't have a clue who I was," I said.

"Yeah, you did," said Marty. "So are you telling me you finally figured it out?"

"No; I haven't," I said. "And that's maybe the one and only thing I have figured out. That there's no way to figure it out, to know who we are. I've heard before that an ocean is constantly changing, and that you can't step into the same one twice. But we're constantly changing, too, and the same person can't step into an ocean twice, either," I said.

"Much deeper, grasshopper," said Marty. "So what does that mean, what are its applicable uses in life, and how can we fit it on a piece of paper small enough to fit inside a fortune cookie?"

"I guess it's just that it doesn't matter who you were, because that was someone else; whether you liked them or hated them, they're out of your life forever, as long as you let them go. And sitting around trying to plan who you're going to be next is just plain stupid, since you have no control over who's coming to call," I said. "So just let yourself come and go, and don't sweat it if you're a loser, idiot, asshole, or all three from time to time, 'cause you'll soon be gone. It's only a temporary state, and another you is right around the corner."

"And that's it? That's the simplest you can make your philosophy? It's still going to have to be one helluva big cookie," said Marty.

"That's it," I said. "So you better get baking."

"Well, I for one am so relieved that you're a different person now; one who doesn't think too deeply about things," said Marty, smiling coyly.

"Are you being sarcastic?" I said.

"Of course," said Marty. "Maybe you're a different Jack than the Jack I used to know back in Minnesota, and all the other Jacks that have come in between. You might like limbo more than football now, or jerk seasoning more than buffalo..."

"The jerk and buffalo are tied," I said.

"Whatever. My point is, you're still *a* Jack even if there will never be a *the* Jack. And no matter how much they may all say they don't, all the Jacks think. A lot," said Marty. "And if you ever need the proof again, just give me a call, because you're so easy to bait into one of these asinine convoluted conversations it's not even funny."

"Remind me again sometime why I ever hung out with you," I said.

"Which one of you?" said Marty. "And which one of me?"

"I'm not going to hear the end of this for a while, am I?" I said.

"Not you, no, because you'll be gone in a minute, but maybe one of the later in the week Jacks will hear the end of it when one of the Martys gets bored with it," said Marty.

"One of me can hardly wait," I said.

Chapter Twenty-One
"Stranded On A Sandy Bar."

The next afternoon Marty and I were sitting on a couple of folding chairs on the beach of di Isla De Luis, our busy time finished at last. The only thing left to do was wait, and that waiting was accompanied by a couple of well earned cold Coronas from the cooler between us.

"See? I told you it would be worth it," I said.

"I never said it wouldn't be worth it; it was just a lot of work, and I'm on vacation," said Marty, taking a sip from his frosty bottle.

"Yeah, sorry about that, but it couldn't be helped," I said. "A lot to prepare."

"Can you at least tell me what this is all about, now?" said Marty.

"Not until the other guys arrive," I said.

"You're such a dork," said Marty.

"Guilty. Anyway, they're here, or will be in a minute. See?" I said, pointing out to sea.

The Lazy Lizard, Crazy Chester's old charter fishing boat, had just come around the southeastern part of di island and into view.

"Finally," said Marty.

"We've been sitting here for all of five minutes!" I said.

"Yes, and I hate waiting," said Marty.

"Ya gotta get your mind around the fact that there is no waiting on di island. What could you be waiting for? You're already here. People spend their whole year waiting to get to places like this, to sit and do nothing. And basically that's all waiting is," I said.

"So people spend good money to fly down here just to wait?" said Marty.

"No, I just said that-" I looked at Marty. "Forget it; it's not going to work. You're not going to suck me into another lame discussion about nothing."

"Fine; I'll just do some of that waiting you said doesn't exist down here for another Jack to come along who I can bait into babbling," said Marty.

"Good; just leave me out of it," I said, standing up to go meet the boat.

A short time later Chester, Gus, Roger, Pat, Cavin, Ernesto, Jedidiah, Boyd, Black Dog, Moon Man, and even Mr. Wonbago stood on di Isla De Luis with us, a pile of their gear nearby. Willie was there, too, but he wasn't going to be there for very long.

"We're here now; can you tell us what the hell this is all about?" said Gus.

"First, I want to thank you all for coming," I said. "And for clearing your schedules for a couple of days."

"You're lucky I just hired a couple of new people," said Chester. "But I notice Francis didn't come."

"No, he refused to be gone that long; you know him and his bar," I said. "He *is* the Monkey."

"Must be his drool, then, too," said Boyd.

"Lovely thought," I said. "Anyway, you're probably all wondering why you're here."

"No, I just got through asking you what this was all about for the hell of it," said Gus.

I ignored Gus being Gus and continued. "I'd like to welcome you all to di Isla De Luis, and my official bachelor party!" I said, as enthusiastically as looking at Gus's sour puss allowed.

"Bachelor party!" said Pat. "I didn't think you were getting married for another year."

"I'm not," I said. "But I wanted to have my party now."

"Any good reason why, before I go get back on the boat?" said Gus.

"Because things are changing so fast around here; who knows where we'll all be a year from now," I said.

"And you invited me to your bachelor party, too, man?" said Moon Man. "Dude, I'm honored!"

"Well, I definitely wanted Black Dog to come, and if you're a friend of his, I want to get to know you, too," I said.

"Careful; he's usually serious about things like that," said Black Dog. "In no time he'll be pestering you, too."

"So what's di plan?" said Roger. "Why are we here in particular?"

"Because this is where the party is," I said.

"Here? On this godforsaken little rock? For two days? I'm going to feel like a castaway," grumbled Gus.

"That's the point," I said. "And it's hardly a rock. It's a nice little island, and I brought everything we need. And if there's anything else we might want-"

"-like a ride home?" said Gus.

I ignored Gus for exactly the five thousandth time, although I didn't know it. "We can call Willie, and he'll run it out to us," I said. "I've hired him to be on call for the next couple of days."

"I tink you be out in di sun for too long," said Wonbago.

"Look, it'll be great. A bunch of guys hanging out on the beach with just the basics; no tourists to pester us, nothing to think about but having a good time. It'll be like back when I first came to di island," I said.

"You know, you're lucky you didn't tell us ahead of time, or we might not have come," said Pat.

"That's why only Chester knew, and only then because we needed his boat," I said. "But I knew he'd be up for it, if he could get away. *He's* still a fun guy."

"I'm totally up for it, too," said Moon Man. "Being one with nature and communing with your fellow man, man; what could be better?"

"So can Willie be on his way, or do I have to face down a mutiny?" I said.

"We be all good, Jack," said Roger. "Anyone here who isn't can just deal wit it."

"I'll keep that in mind," said Gus.

"Roger ees right; boss is throwing us a party, and some of you are whining about eet," said Ernesto. "When was the last time we all were together like thees? And it might be the last time."

"I'm not whining about the party; I'm whining about it being here," said Gus.

I walked over to the cooler and got out a Corona, opened it, then went over and handed it to Gus. "And now?" I said.

Gus took a drink, and said, "What was I talking about again? You heard Ernesto; let's get settled in."

A few hours later, the Magnificent Seven times two minus one were sitting on the beach, the grill cooking up some blackened fish and chicken. We'd just watched the sun sink down behind di island, which was a new experience for most of us.

"You know, I haven't seen di island from this point of view for a long time," said Pat. "Since I arrived, actually."

"It is kind of fun to watch di shoreline," said Jedidiah. "I just wish I could see it better."

"Here, lad," said Black Dog, and he tossed his spyglass to Jedidiah.

"Thanks, Captain," said Jed. He put it up to his eye and studied the horizon. "I can see di Innkeeper dancing happily in di sand, a tiki torch in his hand."

"Why's he doing that?" asked Boyd.

"I don't know; maybe because Crazy Chester's be on fire," said Jedidiah.

"What!" said Chester, leaping out of his chair.

"Just kidding, mon," said Jed.

"Don't do dat; he be paranoid enough already about Francis striking while he be gone," said Roger.

"Yes, I be," said Chester, settling back into his seat.

"How's the food coming?" asked Marty. "I'm starving, and if I don't eat something soon I'll be doomed. I'm not on as much of a familiar basis with alcohol as the rest of islanders."

"We're complete strangers," said Boyd.

"Okay, except for Boyd," said Marty.

"We be pretty friendly, dat be for sure," said Roger.

"He's a good crew mate, and we've served together for a long time," said Black Dog.

"We're downright soul mates," said Gus, holding up his glass of Captain Billy's Black Dog Rum and gazing at it lovingly. "What about you, Jack?"

I looked at my Pickled Parrot, scooped fresh from the wash bucket of them sitting nearby, wapatui style. "I don't know; I can't tell if I'm using her or she's using me, but neither of us cares; we're getting our share."

"Food?" said Marty. "That was my question, in case you've all forgotten."

"Just a few minutes more; you can't rush perfection," said Moon Man, who had volunteered to man the grill. Evidently he'd also spent some time doing just that in Key West, working in a bar he couldn't remember the name of.

"Did you bring your guitar, Cavin?" I asked.

"Yes, I did," said Cavin.

"I can't wait for Kumbaya by the fire, followed by smores and ghost stories," said Gus.

"If there be any ghost stories told, they better be about yours truly," said Black Dog.

"If this was any kind of bachelor party, we'd have naked hula girls to look forward to," said Gus.

"How do you know we don't?" I said.

"Just a wild guess based on the fact that you're you," said Gus. "We'd have a better chance of naked mermaids swimming up and doing an oceanic burlesque show for us."

"Are there any mermaids who *aren't* naked?" asked Cavin.

"There's a few near Madagascar that had the misfortune of running into a skin diving catholic missionary," said Gus.

"I met me a mermaid once," said Black Dog. "Off the shores of Cuba. Jumped right into me boat one night."

"What happened?" I asked.

"Let's just say you've got more cousins than ya think ya do, laddie," said Black Dog. "About three thousand of them."

"I'm not putting them all on my Christmas list," I said.

"Why? You could just buy them one of those bubbling treasure chests and they'd be happy as clams," said Boyd.

"Or a Greek arch to swim through," suggested Cavin.

"Where is di lovely and wet lady now?" asked Roger.

"Up above Crazy Chester's front door. That's what happens to them if they're out of the water too long, contrary to popular belief," said Black Dog.

"You mean, dey don't sprout legs, mon?" asked Jedidiah.

"No; why would they? And where would they be sproutin' from?" said Black Dog. "They aren't some Darwinian super speedsters."

"Well, if she didn't grow di legs den how did you and she...never mind. I don't want to know dat," said Wonbago.

"That's sad, the senorita's all dried out now," said Ernesto.

"Not really, mate; all ya have to do is throw her back in the water and she'll come back to life again, good as new," said Black Dog.

"Great; thanks, Black Dog," said Chester, glumly. "I can't wait for the next time a bunch of these idiots get looped and steal my mermaid and toss her in the ocean to see if you're telling the truth."

"You're welcome," said Black Dog.

"Food's up," said Moon Man. "Come and get it!"

There was a general stampede to the buffet line, led by Marty. I decided to sit back and wait until everyone else went through, and hope that there was still something left to eat by the time I got there. If not, I might have to try and lure one of my cousins into shallow waters for a man sized fillet.

So far, I couldn't be happier with my little party; rum, cooked animals, bullshit by the ton. All I wanted was some camaraderie, and time alone with my friends. If you could actually ever be alone with a dozen compadres by your side.

They were just one of the many things in life that got taken for granted, those friends. You often didn't know how important they were to you until they were gone, and by then it was too late. A good friendship is something you hardly ever have to think about, and that's why it's so important to keep.

And I had so many to care for I wished I could build a preserve to keep them all safe and warm.

Chapter Twenty-Two
"Beach Bar On Di Moon."

Being with a bunch of friends is a wonderful thing.

Being with a bunch of friends around a bonfire is a very wonderful thing.

Being with a bunch of friends around a bonfire on a beach needs to have some new words invented if you're ever going to describe it properly.

All we were really doing was sitting and talking. We had music coming from the boombox I'd brought along, and every once in a while Cavin would pick up his guitar and strum a song or two. But other than that, there was no outside entertainment to make it fun.

Okay, besides beer and rum, that is, and I'm pretty sure they added to the general positive mood of our circle, too. But other than that, we could have been a bunch of cavemen sitting around discussing the day's hunt and who was the cutest cavegirl tourist we'd ever seen on di island. It was back to basics, and basic was good.

It was actually kind of odd that sitting on little Isla De Luis with its smattering of palm trees and Mother Ocean on all sides, almost outdid di island in the way of pure tropical beach aesthetics. And having the moon low in the sky to the east, sparking the ripples in the water, and di island to the west, with its colorful lights all along entertainment row, added even more enchantment to the setting.

In fact, the dangerous little thought that had buried itself in the far reaches of my mind a while back had emerged once again. I couldn't help thinking what a great place di Isla De Luis would be for the most basic of island beach bars. The kind of place you just stumble across and go, *"wow!"*, and rush to a bar stool as quickly as you can. If there even are such luxuries as bar stools present.

Since it would be sitting unprotected way out on a tiny island by itself, it would have to be built like a kid's clubhouse, the kind of structure a Survivor cast member would laugh at as being too crude to suit him. That way it wouldn't matter if a hurricane or boatload of spring breakers decided to knock it down; you'd just throw it right back up again in a day or two. And that would just make it all the cooler looking.

I didn't know if I was actually serious about it, but I could tell already it was going to be hard not to do it. Maybe I could start it up and let some other enterprising islander take over, but either way it was just too fun to fantasize about. I know how excited I would be to be boating around di island and hear good reggae music coming from somewhere, and to turn and

186

look and see this ramshackle structure sitting on a little archipelago. And then the sheer joy of just sitting there for a few hours in the middle of nowhere, a thousand miles from the ordinary.

If I didn't go ahead and do yet another crazy thing, people would never have that experience, and I'd be remiss in my duties as a properly de-evolved human to provide such rum memories. Opening the factory had been one of the greatest things I ever could have done in my life, and this could be something similar, on a much smaller scale. So it was something I would have to give some serious thought to.

Or not.

"Is this island part of our territory?" I asked.

"Dis little ting?" said Wonbago.

"Yeah," I said. "Dis little ting."

"Ya, di island owns it," said Wonbago.

"Then I want to buy it," I said, barreling right along, and leaving my serious thought stranded on the side of the road with its thumb out.

"What for?" asked Roger.

"Does it matter?" I said.

"Actually, it do," said Wonbago. "We be di island council now, remember? We have to decide if it would be good for di island."

"Not yet, you're not," said Gus. "Ya still got a few more days to wait before you get to start making people miserable."

"Anyway, it wouldn't matter either way," said Pat. "If Jack wants this little island, he can have it as far as I'm concerned."

"Fine by me, too," said Roger.

"Wait a minute, mon!" said Wonbago.

"All those in favor of selling di Isla De Luis to Jack, say aye," said Pat.

"Aye!" said Chester.

"All those on di island *council* in favor say aye," said Pat.

"Oh," said Chester.

"Aye," said Roger.

"Aye," said Pat. "Motion carries."

"Hey! I didn't get to vote," said Wonbago.

"It doesn't matter; do the math," said Gus.

"I want my vote," said Wonbago, stubbornly.

"Fine; Councilman Elect Wonbago, how do you vote?" said Pat.

"Nay," said Wonbago.

"Motion carries, in spite of Wonbago trying to be an ass," said Roger. "One beer each a fair price for di sale?"

"Sure," I said, getting up and heading to the cooler before anyone could change their minds.

"Dis is not how we are gonna do tings once we get into office, I hope," said Wonbago.

"Nope," said Pat.

"Good," said Wonbago.

"We'd wait for him to bribe us with the beers first and then give him the island," said Pat.

"Crap," said Wonbago. "I'm gonna need another drink."

"I'm bringing you a beer," I said.

"I don't want no damned beer!" said Wonbago. "Maybe my vote can't keep us from selling you dis island, but I want a Pickled Parrot for it, den!"

"Coming right up, Councilman Elect," I said.

"Dat be better; no one ever gives me di respect I deserve," said Wonbago.

"Maybe dat's because you always act like such a stuff shirted jerk," said Roger.

"No, I don't tink dat's why," said Wonbago. "Although dat's a good reason, too."

I served my payola, and sat back down. All of a sudden I'd committed to opening a beach bar, even though I didn't have a clue how I was going to actually go about it. But paltry things like plumbing and refrigeration wouldn't stand in my way; I had a dream, and that dream was to provide a spot for people to add a unique verse to their songs. There was no higher calling than to do something that would become a part of a great memory for someone, and I'd gladly hand out notes and lyrics to help. And besides, it would be a helluva lot of fun.

It also occurred to me that just as suddenly, I now owned an island. It may not have been that much of an island, but it was still an island. And that was almost even cooler than owning a rum factory; well, almost.

It was so cool in fact, that I immediately felt guilty about getting it so cheap, and I decided I'd do something for di island to make up for it. Billy had already told me he wanted me to have any money he got for the treasure; he said he'd just end up leaving it to me anyway, so I might as well have it now while he was still alive and haunting. I'd already planned on buying him every piratey thing I could get my hands on, especially a new wardrobe, but I hadn't had a clue what I was going to do with the rest of the plunder. But I knew now; a big chunk of it would go to di island school. It was only right; I'd done nothing to earn it, other than being awakened way too early a couple of times by an overzealous Aussie. I only needed so much, and I already had my factory, hut, island, and friends. And Kaitlyn.

Kaitlyn. It seemed I'd just decided to buy an island and open a tiki bar upon it during my bachelor party. Maybe not as big a premarital sin as sleeping with a mermaid stripper the night before your wedding, but it was something I possibly should have talked over with the flip to my flop. Luckily my hula girl was easy going about such things, and if worse came to worse, I could always get it started and pass it on to someone else, as I'd already calculated.

But that was enough calculating for one night. I was still at a party, and it deserved my undivided attention. Marty was here, as were most all of my friends (the cave*man* ones, anyway). The weather, island, and Mother Ocean were here, too, and they were as beautiful as always.

And Mr. Wonbago was dipping into the Pickled Parrots, so things were bound to pickle up.

Chapter Twenty-Three
"I Live On A Diminutive Round Ball."

"Where di hell is my glass?" said Wonbago, whirling around unsteadily in every direction at once.

"It's in your hand," said Cavin.

"What di hell is it doing der?" said Wonbago.

"I'm sure it's wondering the same thing," said Marty.

"Outta di way; I need another Packled Pirrot," said Wonbago, stumbling towards the bucket.

"If he throws up in there I'm not going to be happy," I said.

"Naw; he always passes out first," said Gus. "I give him about ten minutes."

"Hopefully he'll do it out of the way this time," I said.

"He'll drag pretty easy in this sand, anyway," said Gus.

"I'll leave that to you, then," I said.

"Why? Boyd's di island cemetery caretaker; he can deal with the body," said Gus.

"Fine; I just don't want to be tripping over councilmen everywhere I step," I said.

The party had reached its later, chaotic stages. Some people were sitting around the fire, some were meandering around chatting, while others danced around the fire to Marley. Jedidiah and Ernesto had gone to bed in tent and hammock, but Pat hadn't made it that far, and was laying on his back in the middle of the sand, peacefully snoozing.

And then there was Chester, who was standing on the beach with a big flashlight, pointed at his bar. I walked over to see what he was up to, and found him clicking it on and off.

"What are you doing?" I asked.

"Talking to Akiko," said Chester. "We're doing Morse code."

I looked at the shore, and saw a blinking light on the beach in front of Chester's. "What are you two chatting about?" I said.

"I just asked how it went at the bar tonight," said Chester.

"And what did she say?" I said.

"I'm not sure; either pimples were very harpy with the nude Popeye chicken ropes, or purple weighs very heavy when the new papaya chicken raps," said Chester. "You know how fast Akiko talks; I can't keep up."

"Ever hear of cell phones and texting?" I said.

"Heard of 'em, yes. Ever used 'em, no," said Chester.

"Good man," I said, patting him on the back. "I'll leave you to it, then."

I decided to go talk to Moon Man, if he wasn't floating around in the cosmos with Carl Sagan. I found him sitting in the sand next to Billy on the opposite shore, the waves lapping over their toes. I went and sat down between them, refilling my Parrot on the way.

"What's going on, guys?" I said.

"We were just talking about how if we could walk on water we could go on walkabout and follow the islands right on over and down to Venezuela," said Moon Man.

"That would be an interesting hike; with the waves it would be like wandering through the Alps, except they'd be moving," I said.

"It'd be like walking on hyperactive Jello," said Moon Man. "Mm....I love Jello."

"I'm surprised you didn't bring your first mate with you, Black Dog," I said.

"Sam didn't want to come; he had a hot date with that Scottish wench," said Black Dog.

"Scottish wench...you mean, Henri's Terrier?" I said.

"Aye, that's the one," said Black Dog.

"Does Henri know his ward's seeing a pirate?" I asked.

"I don't think he'd mind if he did know; all Cajun's are pirates at heart," said Black Dog.

"I thought he was Creole," I said.

"Don't start again, lad; you're never gonna get it right," said Black Dog.

"Then let's talk about something different," I said. "What was it like for you two being in Key West in the old days?"

"Aw, man! It was glorious," said Moon Man. "The vibes were so totally positive. Just a hodgepodge of everything groovy all on one little island. Music, food, adventure, art, and cool, interesting people; and lots of sex, too."

"I guess you'd have to put sex in with the rest of the good stuff, too," I said.

"I do," said Moon Man. "And drugs. There were a *lot* of drugs, man."

"And that was good?" I said.

Moon Man shrugged. "It was what it was; just a part of the scene back then."

"Speaking of drugs, I have to ask you guys something, especially you, Billy," I said, using his real name as I did on the rare occasion when I tried to get through to the real him. "Were you running ganja in those days?"

Billy looked at me. "Do you really want to know that, lad?" he said.

I thought about it. "Yeah, I do. I've just always wondered. I mean, I don't care, one way or the other. If you did, I don't think it was such a bad thing; back then, things were different, I know. And I think it would be kind of cool. Having a smuggler for an uncle. Almost like a movie or something."

"Then I guess you're in luck," said Billy.

"You mean, you did?" I said. "I knew it!"

"Of course ya knew it; Luis probably told you. Loved the man, but he never could keep a secret," said Billy.

"So what was that like, running grass through the Caribbean?" I said, excited to have a great story coming my way.

"It was a job, just like any other," said Billy.

"Oh come on!" I said.

"Black Dog's playin' it down; maybe the buying, selling, and profit was like any other business, but you could sure have some groovy adventures while you were doing it," said Moon Man. "A lot more than selling Hoovers door to door, that's for sure."

"I wasn't runnin' grass all over the Caribbean, either, though; just between Jamaica and Key West. At least that's what I should have been always doing," said Black Dog.

"Why, what do you mean?" I said.

"Usually I would just pick up me cargo and run it straight to Key West, then head back here and lay low for a while. Work on the rum factory a bit," said Billy. "Me own Black Dog Triangle, it was. But then one run I decided to come back here after picking up in Jamaica. And that's when it all went to hell, just a little bit north of where we are right now."

"What made you change your route?" I asked.

Billy was quiet for a moment, then said, "I was giving somebody a ride."

"There was someone else on board besides you and Sam when the Rum Runner sank?" I said.

"Aye; and I never found any sign of him after the crash. He was just a lad, a little older than Willie. He'd gotten on the wrong side of some people in Jamaica and was headin' for trouble, so I decided to get him out of there and bring him here to di island where he'd be safe," said Billy. "But it didn't work out that way."

"Do you mind my asking why you didn't just bring him to Key West instead, since you normally would have been heading that direction, anyway?" I asked.

"I didn't want him goin' to the states," said Billy. "The war was still goin' on in Vietnam, and though it wasn't likely he'd get caught up in it since he would have been an illegal, I didn't want him to take the chance."

"I'm sorry; I wouldn't have brought any of this up if I would have known there'd be some bad memories for you," I said.

"It's alright, lad. You didn't know about Joshua; that was his name. Nobody around here except Moon Man knows about him," said Black Dog. "Couldn't bring myself to tell di islanders. But you deserve to know, and I'm glad you do, now. It was a long time ago. He deserved a better fate than Davy Jones' Locker; he was a good kid. But I guess sometimes you can't cheat destiny. You get away from one and another finds ya."

"It wasn't your fault, anyway," I said. "You were trying to help him. You can't help it if that's when a storm came up and you sank."

"Yeah, man; you guys just got caught in the middle of a fight between Mother's Ocean and Earth. Those sisters can really go at it sometimes," said Moon Man.

"I know; I've come to terms with it, for the most part. I lost me ship, me first mate, and Joshua. And me cargo, where all my money was tied up," said Black Dog. "Rough night."

"I'll say," I said. "The roughest."

"But, life goes on, and that's what you have to realize, sooner or later. it doesn't do anyone any good to mope around forever," said Black Dog. "If you're unhappy with your lot, ya need to pick a new life, and set your sails and pursue it."

And that's exactly what Billy had done. While I could understand how losing Sam and everything he'd owned when the Rum Runner sank could have turned him into Black Dog, it made more sense now that I knew about Joshua, too.

You could sit and play what if all day in life; what if the boat hadn't sank, and Billy had eventually gotten all the money he'd been trying to raise and opened the factory himself. Where would I be, now? Back in Key West, probably. Not a bad thing, either, by any stretch of the imagination. But I never would have met Kaitlyn. And I wouldn't be sitting on the beach on di Isla De Luis, which I now owned, next to Billy's Black Dog persona during my bachelor party, learning exactly what had happened to him that had ended up bringing me here in the first place. It was enough to make your head spin. One small boat's sinking altered hundreds, perhaps thousands of people's courses.

You might say that the universe is a huge place, and you'd be right. But it's all a matter of perspective. Maybe it's not so much that the universe is big, but that we are so small, that makes the whole thing such a precious, fragile, chaotic miracle. If you want to try and gain some tropical themed perspective on life and our place in it, imagine this. If you took every grain of sand on every beach on Earth and turned them into stars, you might have a shot at approaching the number of suns in the known universe. So look down next to your beach towel and pick out a twinkling grain; in the grand scheme of things, we're standing on the third even tinier ball rotating around it. And that's probably being generous.

But there's still so much going on on that miniscule little grain, our lives bumping into one another and altering eachother's trajectories. And maybe that's it. Maybe it's not the big things that count; what could be big to a universe this size, anyway? Perhaps it's the little ones. And maybe the smaller it gets the more it matters.

Focus the microscope down on a tiny group of friends or lovers who've found each other, and maybe you've finally discovered the only reason for the entire universe to exist.

And if that's the reason, it's a damned good one, if you ask me.

Chapter Twenty-Four
"Gonna Thank My Lucky Stars."

The next morning brought a cacophony of grumbles from every direction; heads full of aches, no showers, sand everywhere it didn't belong, and hungry bellies. A few ocean baths quieted some of the complainers, and calling Willie and having him bring fourteen breakfasts (including one for himself) out from Henri's shut a few more gobs. Unfortunately, the remaining bunch were only appeased by a ride back to di island with Willie. One day as a castaway was going to be it for Pat, Boyd, Jedidiah, and Wonbago; two had to work, and two had just had enough. Wonbago had in fact had way more than enough, since his head was now apparently as large as the island we were on.

That left nine of us to man the beachhead, and I was happy enough with that. I had sort of expected Gus and Chester to desert me as well; Gus because he was Gus, and Chester because of his bar. But they'd stayed on to rough it out for another day, if you could call what we were doing roughing it.

"You know, there are people who would pay good money to do what we're doing right now," I said.

"Then send one over; he can pay me and take my place," said Gus, who couldn't help doing a little whining even though he'd decided to hang around to the end.

"Willie brought us fresh ice, more fodder for the grill, and extra liquid supplies. I've still got the backup battery for the Frozen Concoction Maker, and he's going to go charge the other one just in case, and run it out here later," I said. "I'm going to go make nine Bloody Marys now, and we should be all set for the day."

"You have stuff for Bloody Marys?" said Marty. "Where were you an hour ago, when I needed one?"

"Busy dealing with everyone's bitches," I said. "So are you saying you don't need one now?"

"No, I definitely still need one; I just needed one before, too," said Marty. "I would have thought tossing my anchor into Mother Ocean would have been a dead giveaway."

"Sorry, I missed that," I said, although I wasn't.

"I hope you're going to apologize to the water and the fish," said Moon Man.

"I already did," said Marty.

"Good dude," said Moon Man. "Anyone want to join Black Dog and me in a solar charge?"

"Does it involve sitting very still and quiet?" asked Marty.

"Yep," said Moon Man. "Pretty much all there is to it."

"Then count me in, as long as an occasional sip on a Bloody isn't against the rules," said Marty.

"No rules, except for not ruining anyone else's karma," said Moon Man.

"I think my stomach is stable enough so I can keep from doing that now," said Marty.

I mixed up the Bloody Mary's and passed them out, then sat down to savor my own. Judging by Sol's location in the sky, it had to be somewhere in the noon to one o'clock range already. I guess time flies when you're recovering from rum, too.

"Anyone have any ideas on how to spend the day?" I said.

"It's your party," said Gus. "If you're going to leave it up to me, I'll suggest something like pin the tail on the bachelor."

"I might point out that you're a bachelor, too," I said.

"Maybe not for long," said Gus.

I almost did a spit take with my Mary. As it was, it slowed me down long enough for Roger to exclaim something first.

"You're getting married?" said Roger. "I don't believe it."

"I didn't say I was getting hitched for sure; just maybe," said Gus.

"To who?" said Cavin.

"Si, I'd like to know who's crazy enough to marry an hombre like you," said Ernesto, making as close to a smart ass comment as a guy as nice as he was is able.

"You remember that trip I took last summer to go to my brother's wedding?" said Gus.

"You mean, the selfish, stingy, rich, s.o.b. you can't stand, that paid for your whole trip, including putting you and the entire wedding party up in Hawaii?" said Chester.

"That's the one," said Gus.

"Yeah, what a jerk," said Chester.

"Anyway, I met a nice lady on the beach one night who lives there," said Gus. "I was just going past her home down the beach from the hotel after the reception, and-"

"Were you naked?" I asked.

"Why the hell do you ask me that?" said Gus.

"Because every time I throw a beach party, you end up naked, so I assumed this was no different," I said.

"I wasn't naked last night, was I?" said Gus.

"No, and thank you for that," I said.

"Then can I continue?" said Gus.

"Be my guest," I said.

"Thanks," said Gus "So I ran into the water in front of her house, and she saw me and came down to yell at me, and one thing led to another and..."

"So you *were* naked, weren't you?" I said.

"Yeah," said Gus. "But I wasn't at the time in my story when you asked me; I took off my clothes after that in front of her place."

"Classy," said Cavin.

"It worked, didn't it? I didn't even know there was a woman there, but it must have been fate, because we spent the rest of the week together. And we've been in contact ever since," said Gus.

"I thought you said you were never going to get married," I said. "What's different about this woman?"

"She's rich, for one thing," said Gus.

"Dat explains it, right der," said Roger.

"I can't do this forever; I'm gettin' tired of lugging tourists around. And it's gonna be tougher finding fares once the airport opens up," said Gus. "And I like Hawaii."

"Is there any part in there where you want to marry her because you love her or something?" I asked.

"Might be," said Gus. "But I'm sure as hell not tellin' you lot."

"Well, I guess we have another reason to celebrate," I said. "Although if you leave, it wouldn't be the same around here without you."

"Don't go gettin' all mushy now; I haven't even said I'm leaving yet," said Gus. "And she'll still have to say yes if I do ask her, and what are the odds she's gonna want a crusty old bugger like me?"

"You're not that old, senor Gus," said Ernesto.

"I'm gettin' there," grumbled Gus. "And like Indiana Jones said, it's not the years, it's the mileage. And boy, have I put on the miles."

"Yes, you certainly have," I said. "Never mind treating your body like a tent; you treat yours like a frat house."

"Best way to meet sorority girls," said Gus.

We sat around drinking and mixing Bloodys for a while, just chatting amongst ourselves. Being who I was, I couldn't meanwhile help but think again about the random chance of it all. Gus had spent his whole life alone, and maybe for the most part he'd wanted it that way. But then his brother decides to get married in Hawaii, and stay at a particular hotel, and Gus finally meets the one woman for him, thousands of miles from his natural habitat, and at the right time. And his brother had to meet two other women, fall in love, and get divorced twice before he could fly to Hawaii to marry yet a third.

I guess the odds of everything we end up doing in life are simply astronomical, given the many possible outcomes. The paths all we human's lives take must look like a ball of seven billion tangled strings of Christmas tree lights, and every once in a while we manage to get plugged in to one another. And that's when the good stuff usually happens.

"I'm glad I found you guys," I said, suddenly.

"What?" said Cavin.

"I'm happy I met all of you," I said. "I don't know what brought each of us to where we are today-"

"I think it was your incessant whining all week about some kind of an important get together out here," said Gus.

"I meant, what brought us all to know each other!" I said, somewhat irritably. "To lead us to somehow end up meeting one another. I'm glad it happened, whatever it was. I can't imagine what life would be like without you guys, and we don't always take the time to say how important the people in our lives are to us. So I want to say, thank you, now, while I have the chance."

"Den, on behalf of everybody else here, you're very welcome, Jack," said Roger.

"And while I have the chance, let me say that I knew it was only a matter of time before you started gettin' all weird and sappy again, Jack," said Gus.

"He does do that, doesn't he?" said Chester.

"Yeah, and he better be finished, 'cause I'm not stayin' here if we're gonna start having Hallmark moment after Hallmark moment," said Gus.

"Don't worry; I'm done," I said.

"Good," said Gus. "Now what?"

"Let's party," said Cavin.

"How about we fish instead," said Gus.

"Really? *You* don't want to drink?" I said.

"I didn't say I wasn't going to drink," said Gus. "I just think we should fish, too. That is why we brought all the gear, isn't it?"

"Fishing sounds good to me," said Chester.

"Fishing it is, then," I said.

A beach, the sun, a fishing pole, some suds; and a bunch of good friends. I'd forgotten just how perfect perfection could be.

And just how easy.

Chapter Twenty-Five
"Flip-Flop Children In The Rain."

Seven hours, seventeen fish, and seventy jokes, stories, and anecdotes later, the sun was gone below Mother Earth's horizon. Not that we'd been able to watch it disappear behind di island this time; a bank of clouds had rolled in and obscured our view of anything sky related but them. Cumulonimbi could be extremely selfish attention divas when they wanted to be.

That wouldn't have been so bad, although not being able to look up at the stars on a tropical night is always disappointing. But when the puffy cargo ships in the seas above us decided they'd spent enough time carting the water in their holds around and decided to dump it, that's when things definitely took a soggy turn for the wet.

In spite of a mobilization that would have made General Patton proud, by the time Willie arrived and we'd loaded all the cargo on the Lazy Lizard, we were good and drenched. I could tell this wasn't one of those just dropped in to say hello sprinkles that quickly moved on down the road; this was a hello remember me, I'm the cousin you hate and I'll be staying for a day or two steady downpour.

It's a not so sad and simple truth; it rains in the Caribbean, too. Obviously; it wouldn't be so lush and green if it didn't. And it can do so just as unexpectedly as anywhere else, and just as inconveniently. But sometimes it can even be a welcome break from the norm, unless you're a tourist on a tight schedule trying to fulfill a prescription for UV rays. I'm not sure I would have called this particular session of liquid moonshine welcome, but when all was said and done and we were finally resettled and relatively dried off in the friendly, cozy, confines of the inside bar at Monkey Drool's, I didn't really mind it.

The Shrunken Head Lounge usually didn't get a lot of use; the Innkeeper didn't even open it most days, sticking with the back beach bar unless it looked like it was going to rain for hours. He'd been talking about finally hiring someone else to man it full time though, and to help out around Monkey Drool's in general. The simple fact was that Francis had always been too cheap to dish out even a minimum wage to someone out of his bar's income. But business was good these days, and we'd finally convinced him that it would be worth it to have enough help to at least serve everyone at a pace that wasn't too slow even for di island.

The inner bar hadn't changed much since my fondest rum memory of the place, the year I'd first come to di island, when a bunch of us had holed up there for a hurricane party. I'd gone outside that evening, faced down the storm, and declared my love

210

for Isabella; right before almost getting brained by a falling palm tree. So I suppose I'd come full circle, back at the Shrunken Head Lounge and in love again, only this time it looked like it might stick.

Marty, Roger, Gus, and I were sitting in a relatively quiet corner, the one spot in the bar that was at least a little secluded from everyone else. The rest of my group had taken the opportunity to make their escape, although Chester had said he'd come back from his own place next door if he could. I pretty much figured that meant we wouldn't be seeing him anymore tonight either, but that was fine. My mood had changed along with the weather, and like a soft, steady rain, I was feeling laid back and okay with pretty much any and every little ting that went on.

As I sipped my Toasted Toucan, I tried to spot my shrunken head. The heads were caricatures of di islanders that Jedidiah had painted on coconuts, and Francis had hung from the ceiling of the bar. They used to hang much lower, low enough in fact that you could smack your nose into them if you weren't careful, but I guessed that they'd caused problems when business had picked up, since they were well above our heads, now.

I couldn't find mine; I wouldn't have been surprised if it had been swiped by a tourist and was hanging in someone's den, despite the many signs warning of the dire consequences if you were caught attempting it (keel hauling, voodoo cursing, plank walking, rum and feathering, and of course, the dreaded Pirate's Poison bar shot). I did spot many of di other islander's, though, and Ernesto's noggin' hung right above our table, keeping watch.

The four of us had been a quiet bunch so far this evening; even Party Hardy Marty, who usually kept his inboard motor running at high idle the whole time he was visiting di island, was relatively serene. There hadn't been much conversation, though everyone seemed to be in a good mood. Maybe it was the rain we could hear dripping outside through the open window next to us that was keeping us reserved, but we all seemed content to just sit and be.

"I can't remember the last time I felt this mellow," I said.

"It's probably Moon Man," said Marty. "Right now, he's out dancing in the rain up on Black Dog's Peak, remember?"

"That's right, although I don't know why that would make me feel mellow," I said. "But if I felt like there was any reason to ever move again, I'd think about going up and joining him; a good rain dance might be fun."

"Is he dancing to bring more rain, or to chase away di rain we already have?" asked Roger.

"I think it's more a celebrate the rain we already have dance," I said. "Or an excuse to splash around in the puddles like a kid. Or probably both."

"I like Moon Man," said Roger.

"Me, too," said Marty.

"He's a crazy, burned out old flake," said Gus.

"And?" I said.

"Yeah, I like him, too," said Gus.

"What are you going to do tomorrow, Jack?" asked Roger.

"I don't know; why do you ask?" I said.

"I thought maybe you'd like to ride over on di Crustacean II and visit di Soggy Dollar," said Roger. "You haven't done dat with me in a while."

"Don't you have to turn around and come right back with a boat load of people?" I said.

"Naw; I'll let Sebastian play captain for one more day. You and I can just ride over wit him, and you can get a ride back di next day when I take over again," said Roger.

"I'm game; all I was thinking about doing anyway was getting started on ideas for my bar, but I can do that anywhere," I said. "Especially if I'm sitting *in* a bar at the time."

"Ideas for your bar? What bar?" said Gus. "Now what the hell are you up to?"

"Oh yeah; I forgot to mention. I'm opening up a beach bar on di Isla De Luis," I said.

Gus stared at me. "You're nuts, you know that?" he said.

"Yep; all us good people are. I need something new to fiddle with, and this is it," I said.

"I wondered why you wanted that little island, other than just wanting an island," said Marty. "What are you going to call your place?"

"I don't know; I hadn't thought about it, yet," I said. "That was number one on my list of things to figure out. It should have a name before I do anything else; it'll make it so much easier when I talk about it with people."

"How about Big Kahuna's?" said Roger.

"Or the Green Parrot, after the bar where you started this whole living like a Buffett song deal back in the cities?" said Marty.

"You two are both way wrong," said Gus. "It's got to be Jack's; just plain Jack's."

"I like it," said Marty.

"Yeah, mon, it's very original; I don't know how you came up with it, Gus," said Roger, with a smile.

"Look, if a guy's gonna open up a bar, and especially when a guy from the mainland opens one up in the tropics, he's gotta name it after himself," said

Gus. "And when he has a name like Jack, it's a moral imperative; it's perfect for a bar."

"Thanks, Gus," I said.

"And especially, especially when the place is gonna keep getting destroyed by acts of God and tourism," said Gus. "You want something short so you don't have to keep painting a lot of letters on the new signs."

"True," I said.

"You're gonna need a boat, too," said Roger. "I can help you get one of those."

That thought hadn't occurred to me. I was going to need to be able to run supplies out to di isle while setting it up, even if I let someone else take over and work the place, which was quickly becoming my plan. And you certainly couldn't wade all the way out to di Isla De Luis from di island (not that I'd want to carry stuff through the water), although swimming was possible if not very damned smart, because of the distance.

"I will need some kind of a dinghy, won't I?" I said.

"And a toilet or two," said Marty. "How do you plan on doing *that* without plumbing?"

"I'm working on it, or at least I will be, if you guys give me some time," I said.

"Composting toilets," said Gus. "No plumbing, no muss."

"Never heard of them," I said. "How do you know about them?"

"I get around," said Gus.

"You travel the song lines of toilets, do you?" I said.

"Wherever the air takes me," said Gus.

"Nice smelling air, I bet," said Roger.

"That's maybe one of my problems solved right away, though," I said. "Now all I have to do is keep doing the same ting until der be no problems at all, mon."

"Yeah, you just have to take care of the docks, electricity, refrigeration, construction, etc, etc," said Marty.

"Gives us something to talk about," said Gus.

"All that's a piece of cake compared to the toilets, anyway," I said.

And that was the honest truth, at least up in my mind. Strangely enough, the toilets had been the one thing I'd thought might stand in the way of Jack's grand opening. The rest seemed easy, since I was going to try and make it so basic. Maybe even just beer on ice in some coolers, and a battery powered boom box. That's what I thought of when I imagined Jack's; keeping it simple, stupid.

Sort of like tonight; I'd had grand plans for a crazy last evening of my bachelor party, but here we four survivors sat in the Shrunken Head Lounge, slowly sipping on our drinks, listening to the rain, and talking about my little beach bar, Jack's.

Jack's. Gus was right; it had a nice ring to it.

Chapter Twenty-Six
"I've Got Bars To Build."

A few days later I said my aloha's to Marty once again. Goodbyes with a close friend were never fun, but they were better at least when you knew you'd see them again. And I knew Marty would come back to di island soon; if not for a simple visit, then eventually for my wedding.

Anderton's construction workers had begun clearing trees for the new airport just as I'd begun my own construction project on di Isla De Luis. I was taking my time with mine, not terribly surprising given my normal day to day pace. Each day as I puttered around my little isle like Robinson Crusoe, I'd get help from an unexpected visitor like Boyd, Jedidiah, Willie, or Ernesto. Even Crazy Chester stopped in one day; I guess he needed to pay me back for carting that stick out of his building.

The Anderton folks weren't messing around with their enterprise, though; they were taking down trees faster than a herd of mutant carbon steel toothed beavers. Which was probably due to keeping the construction workers who'd built the resort itself around on di island to work on the airport. And since quite a few weeks had passed between the two projects, they were more than ready to put their people back to work.

The new island council had gone straight to work as well, and it was fairly impressive how much Pat, Roger, and Wonbago had already accomplished in the short time since they'd taken office. Then again, there was a lot they could get accomplished, since they were building an entire governmental structure from the ground up. New laws were soon in place, as was a tiny police force. Nothing so far to keep life on di island from being the easy going, laid back existence that it was, though. In fact, most of the rules they'd made were like fire extinguishers; you tended to forget they were even there, but you'd be glad they were if you needed them. And hopefully, you wouldn't.

There'd been no official word yet from Coop about finding a home for the Roberto Cofresi Billy Danielson Black Dog treasure, just a few quick messages about some promising meetings and negotiations. There was no rush, though; mostly I was just happy the airline hadn't lost it, and that it wasn't now buying case after case of Old Milwaukee Light for a baggage handler in Dubuque.

Otherwise, life continued to breeze along on di island as always. The passing time wasn't marked so much by clocks or even calendars, but by little events such as getting out of bed in the morning, or afternoon, as the case might be. I rarely thought about what day of the week or month it was, unless I was trying to figure out how long it would be before my Kaitlyn would come home to me again.

It was odd how time moved both quickly and slowly on di island. You could sit by the ocean for what seemed to be forever just watching the waves roll in and out, but only an hour or two would have passed when you finally found a reason to move on. Yet on the other hand, someone would suddenly wish me a happy 4th of July, and I'd wonder where the last few months had gone. Just like I sometimes wondered where all the years I've already been on di island have sailed away to.

Not that they haven't been well spent. If they have drifted off without me noticing, it's because I haven't had any reason to keep tabs on them. I wasn't agonizing that I was a year older and nothing had really changed, because there was nothing big I wanted to change. I didn't want a promotion, a new girl, a nicer car, better weather, or more fun. I had what I needed, so it didn't matter if a year or three went by and I found myself in more or less the same boat. I was happy on my little ship, bobbing along mindlessly on a sea of tranquility, and if I could stay on board the same lovely cruise for the rest of my life I wouldn't mind it a bit.

And at least now when I fall into one of my bouts of over thinking things, it's not because I'm trying to figure out how to be happy. Instead, I try to work out why I am happy, which isn't the worst conundrum to have to ponder. It's taken me five or so years to even get to that point, and though I know I have a ways to go, I'm still pleased with my mental progress. Give me another five years and I may not have to think at all.

In that way, I guess I'm going in the opposite direction of di island. It seems I'm de-evolving and gradually becoming more and more simple minded, while di island is advancing with time and growing more complicated. I suppose one day my home will become the archipelago equivalent of modern man, and by then, I'll have returned to the ocean, a happy little bit of floating protoplasm.

For now though, I think we've both arrived at the same position on the evolutionary ladder, some where's down the line from walking upright. I feel in synch with everything around me, like a formerly lost time traveler who's finally managed to pop into his own era once again. That's what I guess we all are; explorers in time, searching for that perfect moment when we know we belong where and when we are. And when we find it, we try and hold on and enjoy it as long as we can, because it may not last forever.

I've been lucky for quite a while now; even when a dark knight has appeared on the horizon and I worry he's going to knock me back into the dark ages, he turns out to be not such a bad guy once you get to know him after all, like the Wind Song Resort. I suppose there's a lot of leeway around here between the good life that we have and a bad one, and it's going to take more that a hotel, road, election, or airport to cause anything heavier than a light sprinkle to rain on my parade. A lot more.

I know my life is going to change when I marry Kaitlyn, and for starters, it won't be quite as simple. It never is when two people are involved instead of just one, but that's okay. There's more than a few good things to make up for the trials and tribulations of disagreeing about where to go out for dinner, like having someone to eat that dinner with. And the same goes for pretty much everything else, including having someone to share the entire crazy life experience with. As Moon Man would say, it's gonna be groovy.

I don't have a clue what's going to happen after that. Or a plan for it, either. The only other thought I've had about the future is asking Kaitlyn if she wants to build a house someday where my beach shack sits now. It just seems like the sort of thing you should do when you get married; I know Isabella had wanted one, and just because my new love has never mentioned it doesn't mean she doesn't, too. It won't be right away, but if she ever gets tired of a tiny two room tiki hut for a home, I'm game to build a bigger nest.

But for the now, I have to hitch a ride to the northern docks with Ernesto in his pickup, to meet a cargo ship. The new toilets for Jack's are supposed to arrive today, and if you can't get excited about new flushers, what can you get excited about? And since it's the last thing I need from the mainland for the bar, I know *I'm* pretty damned excited about their arrival, anyway.

Not as excited as I am about Kaitlyn's pending arrival later this afternoon, but close.

Chapter Twenty-Seven
"Back To Di Island."

"Jack to Willie; Jack to Willie; come back good buddy," I said. "Over."

"Willie here, boss," said Willie. "Over."

"Hey Willie. What's your ten-four; do you have any passengers right now?" I said. "Over."

"I'm just about to drop off a group at Coral Reef Pizzaria. Is there something you need?" said Willie. "Over."

"Yeah, I could use a cold case of Kalik, and you might as well bring me a twelve of Red Stripe while you're at it," I said. "Over."

"I'm on it," said Willie. "Over and out."

I put my walkie down on the bar and sat back on my stool to relax. It had been a busy afternoon and I was running low on a couple of brands, but Willie would arrive by boat in the next hour or so with some fresh supplies. And until then, there were enough other island style choices to get buy.

Today is the grand opening of Jack's. But it's a soft opening, with only some of my islander friends invited. I should have known better; I doubt if a normal day will be as busy as it has been today, and I'd hardly call what I've been doing soft. I keep forgetting that when you invite islanders to a party, they all show up. And they usually bring friends.

But all is well. It's nothing I can't handle, and in the future, you won't usually find me behind the bar if you should stop by, anyway. That's not to say I won't ever be at Jack's, but if I am, I'll likely be sitting on the fun side of the counter.

I will have my single bartending shift a week, though; my new associate Sebastion needs at least one day off now and then. And I know it'll be terribly painful to have to sit on a tropical island and open bottles of beer in the ocean air, listen to music, and gab with people, but I'm willing to sacrifice for the greater good. Just call me Saint Jack.

My friends and I came up with a few great ideas for Jack's that night in the Shrunken Head Lounge, and at the Soggy Dollar the next day. One of the best was using swings instead of bar stools for the customers, something Marty had seen years ago while on his honeymoon in Mexico. One of the biggest advantages was that they'd be a lot harder to chuck into the ocean if you were a drunken tourist happening upon the place while it was deserted, and a lot easier to replace if they did come up missing. And it was pretty cool and relaxing to be able to gently rock your bottom above the sand below you.

Four heavy corner poles anchored in cement, a tiki roof over head, seven swings hanging in the shade in front of the bar, and a couple of tables to set coolers on. Other than the two Jack's signs, one by the dock and one over the swings, there wasn't much else to the place. Except for the music and the outhouses with the new flushers, of course.

We could always add things like hammocks and a few scattered loungers on the beach later, depending. It had all been pretty cheap to throw together, and now I just had to kick back and see what it became; a cool little spot where people stopped in occasionally on their way to somewhere else, or a must see mecca with a waiting line for swing time.

No matter what was to be, Kaitlyn had been all for Jack's, as long as it wasn't going to be a full time gig for me. She herself said she was going to need something to do on di island too, once her one year notice was up at her current real world job. Otherwise, she'd go crazy until she got used to doing close to nothing.

But that was easily solved, too. I happen to know people in high places around here, and di island council agreed with me when I said we could use a tourism czar, and my honey was perfectly qualified. I also thought that would get me off the hook come the next Rum Daze since I figured it would fall under her department's jurisdiction, but Kaitlyn was one step ahead of me and appointed me as her peon handling all things festival related. Oh, well; I'd pretty much known all along going into our coming marriage who was going to be the higher ranking official out of the two of us.

"Nice bar," said Gus. "You do realize how dangerous it is for you to put a place like this where I can easily fly in and anchor within fifty feet of the front door."

"The thought had occurred to me," I said. "But I figured since we didn't serve Painkillers or Parrots that you wouldn't be able to sit here all day without suffering withdrawal symptoms."

"Not yet, you don't; I refuse to believe that you own a rum factory and will never serve rum here," said Gus.

"It is pretty damned sacrilegious, boyo," said Black Dog. "I might have to bring me own bottle next time."

"Yeah, you're gonna be makin' di workers at di factory tink you don't love us anymore," said Faith, as Cavin nodded his agreement.

"Fine; you guys sold me," I said. "I guess since we have ice and limes and pop-"

"You have pop but no rum?" said Gus.

"It was just in case someone stopped by with kids or something," I said.

"You'll have kids but no rum?" said Gus.

"I said you sold me!" I said. "I'll bring out a bottle or two, next time. I'll have to start carting out more ice, too, but I can make it work."

"Good! If you're gonna to have di rum, den you can have fruity cocktails, too," said Faith, since they were her favorites.

"And blender drinks, if you bring out a Frozen Concoction Maker," said Cavin.

"So much for simple," I said. "Next Chester will be telling me to bring out a grill."

"I am kind of hungry," said Chester.

"Then go chew on a coconut; I gotta draw the line somewhere," I said. "By the way, has anyone seen Jolly Roger? He said he'd make it out here today."

"I passed he and Pat on the way here; they said they had to go check out the airport construction site, first," said Ernesto. "Something about a chest the workers dug up out there."

"A councilman's work is never done," I said. "Wait a minute; a chest? You don't suppose Captain Cofresi...never mind. Just if it's anything pirate related, we keep it an island secret; I wouldn't want to make Cooper cry again."

"Speakin' of pirates who aren't here, where did Moon Man take off to?" said Black Dog, searching the horizon.

"Probably off to the cosmos," I said.

"I'm up here," said Moon Man, his voice indeed coming from the great above.

"Where the bloody hell are ye?" said Black Dog.

"I'm up on the roof, man; it's far out up here," said Moon Man. "My connection with Sol is so strong right now; there's lots of good, positive vibes coming from you guys down there, and it's lifting me higher and higher."

"Despite the lack of rum," said Gus.

"Just don't fall through the thatching; it's not that sturdy everywhere up there," I said. The last thing I needed was Moon Man crashing through the roof and falling onto the bar top; it would be a real bummer, dude.

"How did he get up there?" asked Kaitlyn.

"I don't know; he must have used the ladder," I said.

"Chester came and got that yesterday, didn't you?" said Kaitlyn.

"Yeah, I needed it back to hang up a life preserver on the wall that washed up on shore," said Chester.

"Then he must have just levitated," said Black Dog, calmly.

"Does that a lot, does he?" said Cavin.

"All the time," said Black Dog. "I'm always finding him sitting up in a palm tree."

I looked up at the roof and shook my head.

"So what's next, Jack?" asked Cavin.

"What do you mean?" I said.

"What are you going to do next? You've got the factory, the plantation, your hut, the girl, di island, the festival, and now the beach bar," said Cavin. "So what is Jack Danielson going to do now?"

I thought about it, but was quickly reminded that I didn't own a clue. "I don't know, but I'm not going to Disney World, if that's what you're asking," I said.

I reached back into a cooler and pulled myself a frosty Kalik out of the ice, opened it, and stuffed a lime wedge down its throat.

"I guess if I had to say, I'd tell you that all I plan on doing for sure is stayin' right where I am," I said. "And back on di island, of course."

I looked out at the ocean from underneath the thatching that was rustling in the breeze, and took a sip of my beer. There was sparkling, blue green water and good friends in almost every direction. There was even one above my head right now, although I hoped that wasn't going to become the norm. A few drops of water falling onto my head from time to time I could handle. But if it ever starts raining hippies in my tropics, I'm going to contact my nearest island councilman and voice my concerns about climate change.

It was a good opening day for Jack's. As I watched a group of islanders play Frisbee while another congregation bounced a beach ball around, I almost felt like I *should* have brought food out for everyone, to keep the party going all day and into the night. But then that's what I always want to do; keep the party going. Forever, or at least for however long my own song on Mother Earth lasts.

If you can't enjoy your life, then what's the point? I don't really think we're put on the planet for any particular reason, so why not choose your own? Mine is to make myself happy, and one of the things that does so is making sure other people have a good time. Selfish, I know, but that's just the way I am.

Of course, that's not going to stop me from fulfilling my own wants and sipping a Toasted Toucan, digging into a bowl of Henri's gumbo, or just watching the sun sink over a sandy beach. Hell, I might even do all three at once, since there's no good reason not to. But if a Bud Light, a Hungry Man dinner, and C.S.I. on the tube with your honey does it for you, then more power to you; if you're happy, that's all that matters.

Just follow your song and see where it leads; maybe it will be someplace new, or back to your front door. Being alive is a wonderful thing, and wasting your chance at the dance is a cryin' shame since we may not get another.

My own song is a Caribbean tune. If you ever get the urge to get your island on, come on down to Jack's and pull up a swing; you won't regret it.

But if you ever leave to go home from the tropics, be warned.

Sooner or later, you'll just have to go back to di island.

The End

6484724R00136

Made in the USA
San Bernardino, CA
11 December 2013